TWIST

POSITIVE WAY

CHIKAMSO C. EFOBI

First paperback edition printed 2015 in the United Kingdom
A catalogue record for this book is available from the British Library.

ISBN 978-0-9933542-0-5

Published by Doxa Consulting Ltd
For more information about special discounts for bulk purchases,
please email: publishing@doxaconsulting.co.uk
Tel: +44788127142

Website: http://twistedinapositiveway.com
Book cover designed by Adebowale Adesuyan of House of Pictures,
Nigeria
Printed in Great Britain

Acknowledgement

This is to express my profound gratitude to everyone who has contributed to the writing and production of this novel.

To my editor Monica LaSarre, for her brilliant and tireless effort in editing my manuscript.

To Adebowale Adesuyan for taking my ideas and creating the master piece that is this book cover art design.

To my father Elder Uzochukwu Efobi and my mother Barrister (Mrs) Chinwe Efobi for their unwavering support which encouraged me to pursue my dreams.

To my siblings Onyinye, Onyeka and Lotanna for always being so positively excited about this project.

To my friends for the time and effort they spent in beta-reading my manuscript and providing suggestions on my book cover art design.

To Steve Pressfield for his book, "The War of Art" which provided me the needed kick in the backside to get my manuscript finished after procrastinating for 8 years.

Finally to Stuart Thomas who inspired the title for this book.

For Chizoba
(August 24, 1986 – May 28, 1994)

PROLOGUE

May 1994

IT MAY NOT have been an extraordinary sight to most, seeing a 9-year-old in Primary 4 stepping out of an examination hall. However, Adaugo was no ordinary 9-year-old, and writing her common entrance exams in Primary 4 was no ordinary occurrence, at least not where Ms. S.T. Shoniyi, headmistress of Excel Primary School was concerned.

A student of Excel Primary School, Adaugo had fallen under the umbrella of a new rule instated by Ms. Shoniyi. The headmistress banned pupils who were "under-aged" from writing the National Common Entrance exam. Under this rule, Adaugo would have had to wait until Primary 6 to sit for the exam. Sitting for and passing the National Common Entrance exam is a prerequisite for attending junior secondary school.

Ngozi and Obiora, Adaugo's parents, were skeptical about this rule though, especially since pupils who had graduated in years prior to Adaugo's set had sat for the exams in Primary 5 without issue. Mama Obinna, a family friend, had even reported that her son was enjoying junior secondary school and was doing very, very well

1

and he had sat for his common entrance exams in Primary 5!

Adaugo's parents tried to make sense of Ms. Shoniyi's rule, even going so far as to postulate that it was her future income stream she was protecting by requiring students to wait until Primary 6 for their exam. In the end, there seemed to be no rhyme or reason for such a rule, and Adaugo's parents decided to take matters into their own hands, rules or not. In an act of blatant defiance, Adaugo was enrolled in a different state run primary school, one where she would be allowed to sit for her exam in Primary 4. They rationalized that Adaugo could use the exam as a mock trial of sorts, one which would give her opportunity to practice the exam and get a feel for it so that she would know precisely what to expect when she took it again in Primary 5.

This plan made perfect sense to Ngozi. There was no way she was going to allow her daughter to waste one more year in "that school," as she always put it. Her first daughter was almost always at the top of her class, and clearly she was ready for secondary school. Delaying that progress was nothing but a waste of everyone's time.

Adaugo didn't see the situation exactly the same way as her doting mother. She quite liked being the best in her class, and it was flattering to be the class monitor (a position reserved for either the most brilliant pupil, or the oldest and toughest looking pupil). She didn't complain about the new exam rule, not the way her mother did, because being at the top of her class was something she had grown accustomed to, and being the class monitor had its perks. For example, she could write all the names of her enemies on a list, and each would then receive about six strokes of the cane. She didn't write names lightly, truly it was reserved for her enemies – those bigger, older boys who defied her authority by continuing to make noise when the teacher stepped out of the classroom. On some days when the boys got really, really angry at the flogging they received from their teacher, Miss Banke, they would chase her. She in turn would run to Papa Chikata the security guard, waiting at his station until the boys got tired of waiting for her to emerge or until she was picked up from school. On some days, she got lucky and extreme patience wasn't required: Papa Chikata would chase the boys away for her, and Adaugo would stick out her tongue at them all as they scattered.

Undoubtedly, Adaugo was a lively child as much as she was bright. She questioned what was, what wasn't, and why things were or weren't the way she saw them. She feared no one, yet she respected all. If it was her mother who encouraged her to excel in school, it was her father Obiora, a clearing and forwarding agent, who taught and encouraged her to ask questions and speak her mind. As is often the case with parents, a moment arrives when they wonder what they have done, what kind of inquisitive monster they have created, and Obiora was no exception. Sometimes he would grow weary of Adaugo's numerous questions, especially when she continued to stream them in his direction when her father was in the middle of some other task, like tucking in her and her younger sisters, Ifeoma (younger, but only by eleven months) and Obioma (younger also, but by three years and three months).

The bed time routine included a story usually, read to the three girls by their father. More often than not, whatever bed time story Obiora chose to read was interrupted repeatedly so that he could intervene in arguments between Adaugo and Ifeoma. They argued about what story should or should not be read, while Obioma quietly sucked her thumb and watched her two older sisters bicker and argue. Her displeasure with the scene was registered with a sharp, tearful cry when the argument became too loud, too animated, or was simply taking too long to resolve. In these instances, Obioma's cries usually resulted in a near immediate stop to the argument, with the energy of the two squabbling sisters being redirected towards stopping Obioma's crying.

With their patient father doing all he could to peaceably put his three daughters to bed in one room, the girls' one-year-old baby brother, Ugonna, was being rocked to sleep by their mother in another room. Theirs was a busy home, a three bedroom flat in Mushin, a part of Lagos, Nigeria, an area known for being riddled with violence and criminal activity. It was not unusual to hear the sound of someone's tearful wail after being dispossessed of their valuables by armed robbers who operated at night. One of their neighbours was recently a victim.

As she rocked Ugonna to sleep, Ngozi, a trained food nutritionist, elevated her feet which were swollen from pregnancy. As Ugonna drifted off to sleep in one arm, she pulled out her dog-eared law textbook and studied for one or two hours before finally retiring for the night. Ngozi had always wanted to be a lawyer, but had postponed her dream in order to follow her parents' advice. It was the 1970s then, and her parents cautioned that a powerful career path, like law, would prevent Ngozi from marrying "on time," whatever that meant. Instead, she had settled for a career in nutrition, but only after making a promise to herself that one day she would become a lawyer. Now, some twenty years later, Ngozi was still studying to become a lawyer, even while she helped to guide Adaugo through her own education by creating opportunities for her to sit for the common entrance exam as early as possible.

Adaugo emerged from the examination hall. It had been a big day for her, a momentous experience. As excited as she was to learn the outcome of her exams, she was more excited to be able to finally visit her sister in the hospital. Two weeks prior, Ifeoma had fallen ill. Yesterday, she had successfully undergone surgery to correct an intestinal obstruction, a condition which was quite rare in Nigeria but easily treatable with a simple surgical procedure. After the surgery, Adaugo was relieved to learn the procedure was a success, and especially relieved to hear from the doctors that Ifeoma could begin receiving visitors the next evening. Ifeoma would be very tired of course, and her visitors must be very quiet.

Surgery or not, Adaugo could not wait to pull her sister's hair and for them to fall right back into quarrelling, which would feel normal after Ifeoma's weeks of illness. She had missed her sister during Ifeoma's time in the hospital, and was dismayed to learn that Ifeoma was still in some pain and wouldn't be fun to play with again for quite some time. Still, she looked forward to the visit after her exams were done.

Standing outside the exam centre, Adaugo waited for her father's company driver, Uncle Peter, and felt somewhat uneasy. Quickly she dismissed this uneasiness as post-exam jitters and resolved to continue waiting patiently and quietly. In short order, her father's blue Peugeot 504 saloon car pulled into view and Adaugo noticed that, not surprisingly, Uncle Peter looked as grumpy as ever. She greeted him and received the usual muttered, non-committal response in return, though he did manage to remember to ask how her exams went.

"I think I will pass," she said.

Uncle Peter glanced at her through the driver's front mirror and gave her a smile, a sight she had seldom seen, and she thought it odd. Puzzled, she fastened her seat belt and reclined in her seat, waiting for the usual car sickness to strike. At Hare Krishna hill in Oshodi, another less than glamorous area of Lagos, she caught Uncle Peter's gaze once again. He stared at her through the mirror and she smiled back at him, though she continued pondering the reason for such frequent glances. Finally, curiosity got the better of her, and she posed a question to Uncle Peter, hoping it would begin to uncover some answers behind his strange behaviour.

"Uncle Peter? Please, do you know when Ifeoma will be discharged from the hospital?"

"Soon, very soon," said Uncle Peter.

Smiling, though no closer to understanding Uncle Peter's glances, and exhausted from her exams, Adaugo fell asleep quickly in the backseat. After what seemed like only a few moments, she felt the car come to a stop and knew that they must have finally arrived at home and she could tell Mum and Dad all about her first common entrance exams.

She climbed up the four flights of stairs, and her

excitement changed abruptly again to unease. It hit her suddenly, and the closer she got to the door of the family's flat the more intense the feeling became. Again she shook it off and, arriving at the door, reached up to press the doorbell.

The door was opened by Obiageri, the house help, who immediately and excitedly whispered, "Ifeoma is dead!"

Thinking the house help's exclamation some cruel joke, Adaugo admonished Obiageri and sharply warned her never to try such a joke again, and walked into her home. However, as she drew closer to the sitting room, Adaugo could not help but wonder if Obiageri's outburst might actually be possible. She called out to her parents then: "Mummy, Daddy, where is everybody?"

When no one answered her call, her curiosity grew to annoyance. *Why is no one coming to ask how my exams went*?

She carried on, walking through the flat and calling for her family, but with each step and each unanswered call it seemed as though the world was beginning to slow down. And then she saw her pregnant mum, sprawled out on the floor, completely given over to her tears. In that moment, she noticed a number of strange faces in the room as well, and she couldn't understand what was happening. Her head was spinning, her confusion grew, and then, her dad emerged from his room.

"Is it true?" Adaugo asked him. "Daddy, is it true?"

"Is what true?" her father replied.

"Is Ifeoma…dead?"

"Who told you this?"

"Obiageri. Obiageri told me. Please, please, tell me. Is

it? Is it true?"

His one word reply was unnecessary by that point as her mother's tears and the strangers surrounding them told her all she needed to know, but a tearful and weak voice mustered one anyway. "Yes," Obiora replied to his young daughter. "Yes."

Adaugo felt the world spin, faster and faster and faster it spun, pitching her into black silence. Through the deep silence that suddenly surrounded her, she could hear a distant sound of people scrambling around her as her body hit the floor, and her yellow lunch box dropped from her hand.

PART ONE

CHAPTER ONE

CHRISTMAS THAT YEAR didn't feel at all celebratory. Without Ifeoma, the Obi family felt incomplete and dreary. Though the new baby had arrived by then, the joy of giving baby his first Christmas was eclipsed by the sadness of spending their first Christmas without Ifeoma. Even though it was supposed to be a festive time, Adaugo simply couldn't feel festive without her sister.

The year leading up to Christmas had seemed to march slowly by. Normally, Adaugo simply could not wait for public holidays to arrive such as Christmas and Easter and the odd holiday the Nigerian government decided to create for the country on what seemed like a random whim. In previous years, she had excitedly counted down the days until Christmas, tallying how many days were left using the white calendar in the sitting room. She had called her sister Ifeoma then, and asked her to write down the results of the countdown on a black board with white chalk. The process wasn't nearly as straight forward as it sounds, because the figure Adaugo asked Ifeoma to record had to first be verified by Ifeoma.

She would march to the same calendar, prop herself on one of the brown leather seats, leaving an imprint of her dusty foot on the chair, only to arrive at the same conclusion at an agonizingly slower pace. Though Adaugo would scream and stamp her foot with impatience, this simply didn't help Ifeoma hurry. In fact, it had the opposite effect. Ifeoma, distracted by Adaugo's display of impatience, would lose her train of thought and forget where she had stopped counting, meaning she needed to start the entire process all over again.

Typically it was at this point that Obiageri would emerge from her room, eyes red from her clandestine afternoon nap and shout, "*Umazi a, O gini*, these children! What is it? What is the trouble?"

"Ifeoma is wasting my time!" Adaugo replied one day. "I told her there were seventeen days until Christmas, but she does not want to agree! She still insists on counting, slowly!"

Ifeoma's retort was calm and factual. "Yes," she said. "I need to make sure you are correct. Do not think that just because you are older than me that you know everything. I have to count it myself!"

"But you can't even count! Obiageri, you'll see; ask her to count!"

"Ifeoma, count for me, let me see if you are correct," Obiageri said, yawning again.

"1, 2, 3, 4, 5, 6, 7, 8, 9, 10, 12, 14, 13, 16…"

"Jesus, you can't even count! I knew it!" Adaugo was more frustrated than ever. "You can't even count and there you are, wasting my time! Tell her, sister Obiageri!"

Inevitably both girls would turn and look to Obiageri, willing her to step in and resolve their conflict. But

Obiageri would simply gaze back at them and scratch her short hair lazily for ten seconds or so before diverting them: "Ifeoma, look what you did to that chair! Start dusting it, *kita,* right away!"

This usually distracted the two girls sufficiently such that neither realized that sister Obiageri could not count past the number ten herself!

It had been one year since the last time Adaugo and Ifeoma had argued about the Christmas countdown, and this year there would be no argument. Without her partner in crime in tow, Adaugo had to assume the countdown alone, and it simply wasn't fun alone. So she neglected the countdown, choosing instead to spend her time in the company of her books and the characters she met in them. Hopefully they would be entertaining and distract her sufficiently from the sadness she felt.

Sometimes Adaugo would trace the characters from her books onto plain white paper and then embellish them with bright colours and patterns as a gift to her mummy and daddy, hoping the artwork would make them happy. Ngozi would acknowledge her daughter's efforts with a smile and encourage her to do some more. Other times, Adaugo set illustrating aside in exchange for authoring. She wrote her own books, folding a small stack of white printing paper together and holding them in loose binding by tearing the top, left hand corner and folding the torn parts in opposite ways.

With great pride she presented her books to Uncle Nkem whenever he came to visit. Uncle Nkem was Ngozi's elder brother, the closest out of Ngozi's other four siblings. He would arrive with baskets of fruit and Okin shortcake biscuits, which Adaugo loved, and she would attempt to sell her books to him for fifty *kobo*. Uncle Nkem acted as though this were too expensive and then would proceed to haggle the price down, and Adaugo stubbornly refused to budge. After a time, he would give in with a great sigh of resignation and relent to buy two of Adaugo's books, which she would turn over to him happily and with a self-satisfied grin. With her hard-earned money, she would proudly deposit her one *naira* into the piggy bank she had devised from an empty cardboard St. Louis sugar box, and then replace the piggy bank in its sitting room cabinet until the next time.

Though she tried to lose herself in her books and considered starting a new authoring or illustrating project, this Christmas just didn't feel the same and she couldn't bring herself to. Even for the family, Christmas felt different. Whereas they had enjoyed a lively gathering to celebrate the holiday in years past, on this Christmas the family sat at the dining table and ate quietly, speaking nothing to one another. Each one of them seemed intent on concentrating their gaze on the brown flower vase with artificial flowers at the centre of the table, as if it was somehow the most interesting sight their eyes had ever met.

CHAPTER TWO

May 28, 1995

I T WAS A Sunday, bright and sunny and full of all the promises of a new day. As if it were any other day, Obiora awoke at 6:00 am, nudged his wife Ngozi, and slid out of bed. He walked to the window, a cut-out in the wall surrounded by wood and covered with sheets of woven wire net. The holes in the net were wide enough to let in a breeze of fresh air, yet small enough to keep mosquitoes out. It was there, standing by the window, Obiora remembered this was no ordinary Sunday.

On this day one year prior, Ifeoma had left them. From his perch by the window, he looked back over his shoulder at the bed where his sleeping wife lay, trying to gather as many last moments of sleep before she must awaken and face this day which she dreaded. Obiora sighed. So much had changed in the span of twelve months. He walked across the room to the baby's cot and checked on their little one. He was happy to see that his young son was still sleeping as evidenced by deep and peaceful breaths. Obiora watched the baby's chest and was caught once again by the deep recognition of his late daughter in the tiny face of his new son. It was uncanny how much the two resembled one another. Opening the soft mosquito net which, like the net on the windows, was used to keep out mosquitos, he picked up the baby. The baby's knees jerked slightly as his father raised him from the cot and into his arms, but the baby continued to sleep and remained oblivious to all that was happening around him and how significant this new day was to his family.

His father cuddled him and sang softly into his ear and a smile swept across his face. Obiora's singing woke Ngozi and she sat up, rubbing the sleep from her eyes.

"*O teta go*, has he woken up?" Ngozi asked, her eyes searching her husband's face.

"*Mba, o kana alaru ula*, no, he is still asleep," her husband answered.

"*Ka anyi je kpe epere*, let us go and pray then," said Ngozi.

Obiora gave the baby a soft peck and was greeted with the same smile. He put the baby back in his bed and replaced the mosquito net while Ngozi tied her head scarf and picked up her Bible and red tambourine. As they both left the room, she left the door ajar in order that they might hear if the baby awoke.

Obiora walked through the house playing the tambourine, waking the entire family with the exception of the baby. Each person came out of their rooms in different states of alertness, some still quite sleepy, Bibles in hand. The girls tied their head scarves. They all converged in the sitting room and started singing and clapping, praising God. Even though everyone tried to be cheerful, the significance of this day was not lost on the family, and Ifeoma's absence seemed even more evident that day than others. No one averted their gaze to avoid looking at the seat which used to be hers. After the praise session, they all sat down and Obiora opened his Bible reading guide to the day's reading assignment and shared the Word.

"Let us open our Bibles to Joshua 24:14-15," he said. Then, he read aloud:

> *"So honour the Lord and serve him wholeheartedly. Put away forever the idols your ancestors worshipped when they lived beyond the Euphrates River. But as for me and my family, we will serve the Lord."*

As he finished reading, the family waited patiently for him to announce the next passage they would read. But he didn't speak. Instead, Obiora sat still, silent, staring at his Bible study guide. Ngozi leaned over and watched as Obiora pointed to the study guide. He didn't speak, or couldn't speak, all he could do was point to the lines that he had just read to himself. She looked uneasy as she took the guide from him and opened her own Bible to read the passage her husband had highlighted. First she read the words to herself, without making a sound. Then, sighing deeply, she looked at her husband and then slowly began reading the words to her family, aloud, as her eyes filled with tears.

"1 Thessalonians 5:18," she read aloud:

> *"Be thankful in all circumstances, for this is God's will for you who belong to Christ Jesus."*

As Ngozi read the words, Adaugo observed that her father seemed lost in thought. She wondered if he was pondering the immensity of the words which were so profound and yet so perfect for their present situation.

CHAPTER THREE

T HAT EVENING THE family returned to their flat from their place of worship. Visitors and well-wishers returned home with them from church, eager to check on the family and share words of encouragement on this day of memorial and remembrance. As such, the house was a bee-hive of activities. Visitors traipsed in and out and extended family members were on hand to serve the visitors and help care for and watch over Adaugo and her siblings.

As evening drew to a close, the visitors started to leave. Eventually extended family members said their good byes, promising to check in more often. As the last member of their extended family left, Adaugo heaved a sigh of relief. At least now she would have the sitting room to herself, she thought, as Obiora and Ngozi retired to their room.

It had been an eventful day, and a noisy one, and Adaugo was grateful for some alone time, finally. She picked up the remote controller, turned the television to NTA 2, Channel 5. It was already 6:30pm and she sat down on the sofa. A half hour later, the network news came on and her parents emerged from their bedroom to join her.

As the newscaster's voice droned on, reeling through headlines and coverage of the day's events, Adaugo dozed off. It wasn't until Frank Olize's voice came on the air to present *Newsline*, a popular NTA magazine programme covering the activities and notable events from the preceding week, that she woke up. Stretching on the sofa, she thought she heard the baby's voice from her parents' room, and so she slid off the sofa and ran to check on her little brother.

She reached his side quickly and was relieved to see that she had heard correctly. The baby was indeed awake. She knelt beside his bed and played with his fingers for a few moments, enjoying the connection with her tiny sibling. Then she decided to check if the baby had wet himself, as she had seen her mum do, and so she extracted her finger from the baby's soft grip, pulled up his shirt and began to gently undo his napkin.

The baby suddenly grew very quiet, exchanging the playful giggles of moments ago for complete silence. She looked up from the napkin at him to see if he was alright, and her gaze passed over his tummy. On it, she saw a line. It looked exactly like a scar Ifeoma had from a previous operation when she was three years of age, and hers was in the same spot on her tummy. She blinked her eyes and looked at the baby, who was now wearing a smile that looked completely out of place, not at all a smile she would expect to see on a baby. She recognized the smile very clearly, however.

Her eyes shot back at his tummy, but the mark she had seen moments ago was gone now, and the baby was again lying quietly, the same way he had only minutes before.

It was in this moment that she knew her sister was alright. As would become her experience in the years that followed, Adaugo was learning to recognize signs of the divine all around her. This instance was one of the first in her life, and she took it then as a simple sign revealing that her sister was at peace and no longer suffering.

Chapter Four

THE BEGINNING OF a new school year found Adaugo as excited as ever to embark on a new journey. Having successfully passed the Common Entrance examinations, she had secured admission into the Federal Government Girls' College Abuloma in Port Harcourt, in the capital of Rivers State in the South-South region of Nigeria.

At ten years old, having never been to Rivers State, she was eagerly anticipating the opportunity to attend boarding school and prove to everyone that she was her own grown-up girl. Although the new experiences gave her reason to be anxious, she did her best not to show it. Instead, she set about the task of demonstrating in big and small ways that she was a mature girl, able to handle herself in all situations. Her first opportunity to set fear and anxiety aside came as she took her window seat in the economy class section of the Albarka passenger plane that would take her to Rivers State.

With the demeanor of one who understood their responsibilities, she fastened her seat belt promptly. Then she looked around for the knob that would allow her to adjust her seat. It was the first time she had been on a plane and adjusting her seat was not something she would normally have thought to do, but she was observing those around her and learning quickly how to demonstrate the new-found maturity she was embracing. So, she mimicked the adults around her, including another passenger who was that very moment adjusting their own seat using a knob, which she too searched for.

First time travelers and experienced travelers alike are not strangers to the wave of insecurity that comes as take-off approaches. Adaugo had a fleeting, insecure thought too, one of seeing her plane crash in her mind's eye. She had seen movies and TV shows where the plot centered on a plane crash and she took a moment to ponder the possibility that this may be the last moments before her life ended. Sensing her anxiety, her father held her hands and together they said a short prayer asking for safety.

"Our Father, as we take off on this journey, please guide the pilot and take control of every part of this plane. Help us to land safely and let our onward journey be one filled with success in Jesus' name, Amen."

After the prayers they sat upright waiting for the plane to take off. The plane began to ascend and she felt an uneasy feeling in her tummy and closed her eyes, waiting for it to pass. Eventually the feeling did pass as the plane levelled itself and found its way through the clouds. She drew open her window curtain and looked out into the clouds. The clouds looked just like cotton wool, the same kind her mum used for cleansing her face at night, and she would have given anything to be able to extend her hand out the window and wrap the billowy white puffs in her small fingers.

Even at the age of ten, Adaugo had a sense within her, something one might describe as a still, small voice that whispered in her heart and guided her through her days. Some might call it spirit or give it the name of a deity, but the name was less important than the fact that Adaugo considered it to be a voice of the divine. She had come to think of this voice as that which belongs to "Herself," and Herself's presence was known in Adaugo's consciousness many times each and every day. In the instant when she wished she could open the plane window and touch the clouds, she wasn't surprised to hear the guiding voice of Herself quickly tell her it would be a bad idea because no one else's window was open, so it was probably not safe. She heeded the voice and settled back into her seat.

Then she sat up and looked down through the window again, this time noticing that houses were beginning to look like the Lego brick houses she had played with as a child. Green patches of farmland carpeted the landscape below, but then the aircraft rose higher and the houses and farmlands disappeared from recognition until she felt as though she was floating in a sea of white and nothingness.

When the plane levelled, the air hostess came around with her trolley to offer beverages to the passengers. Adaugo watched with fascination as the trolley moved ever so slowly down the aisle, and when it finally made its way to her seat she looked at her father to see if he would be okay with her asking for juice. He nodded and she excitedly asked for a glass of orange juice, feeling very grown up. The air hostess handed the drink to Adaugo and smiled at her before moving on to the next seat.

Obiora waited for the air hostess to leave before

saying, "Our rule for not accepting things from strangers does not apply when the air hostess asks you if you want anything. This is because we have already paid for the meals as part of the plane tickets, so feel free to ask for anything you want."

He then went on to tell Adaugo a story about his friend who travelled on an 8-hour international flight without eating out of fear that he would be charged extra for anything he ate. When his friend arrived at his destination, he was surprised to be informed by his host that all the items he had rejected while in the air were already covered by his flight ticket.

Adaugo laughed at this story, not unkindly but from the recognition that, as grown up as she insisted on being, she too might have made this same mistake had her father not guided her through her first flight. She was learning so much, and she felt even more grown up today than yesterday now that she understood the rules of flying and how payment for food and drink worked while on a plane. Every day she was growing wiser.

CHAPTER FIVE

T HEY ARRIVED SAFELY at Port Harcourt airport and then continued their journey by road to Abuloma, a two-hour drive. In the airport taxi, Adaugo and her father reviewed her list of items to make sure they hadn't left anything off. With this activity completed, there was not much more to do on the long car ride other than look out the window and anticipate what was ahead of her. Finally, a maroon-coloured school gate came into view and the taxi driver pulled up to allow them to speak to the security guard, a man in a navy blue shirt and trousers who saw them and walked briskly to meet them from an area in the shade.

"Good evening, *oga*," said the security man.

"Good evening. I am here to drop off my daughter. She is starting JSS1," said Obiora.

"Okay, no problem, sir. Can I see your admission letter, please?"

Her father produced a folder of documents then and handed them to the security man. He cross-checked all the papers while stealing glances at Adaugo to confirm that she bore resemblance to the passport image included in her documents. When he was satisfied that all was in order, the documents were returned to her father and the taxi driver was given a motion to indicate that he should drive through the gates.

Despite the exhaustion she felt from travel, Adaugo was suddenly very wide-awake and eager to see every element of her new surroundings. She gulped up observations from her taxi window, like one with an insatiable thirst, taking in the buildings painted in different colors and noticing their names. She saw Ixora House, Lavender House, Jasmine House, and several older buildings with no sign boards, as well as a lot of grass and trees. The patches of lawn were something she was unaccustomed to, never having seen so much grass in one place her entire life. Finally, their drive was over and the taxi pulled to a stop in front of her hostel.

Obiora exited the taxi and met the driver at the booth of the car to assist in removing Adaugo's things, and carefully he placed her belongings on the coal tar road. Bracing herself for the next leg of her adventure, she eventually slid out of her side of the car, straightened her dress, and walked to the booth of the car to join her father.

Her father spoke a few words to the taxi driver, telling him that he would only be a few minutes, and proceeded to walk Adaugo to the gate of her hostel. Here was another opportunity for Adaugo to hide her anxiety, realizing perhaps for the first time that her father was not staying but for a few minutes to drop her off, and that she would soon be alone. She hid her anxiety behind a question.

"Will you come and visit me every term?" she asked.

"Of course we will," her father replied.

"Will I always go back to Lagos by air then? The

journey here was very quick," Adaugo said.

"Of course, yes. Every single holiday, you will fly back to Lagos."

The thought of seeing her family every three months and travelling there by air didn't seem so bad.

"I will miss you, Dad," she said.

"And I will miss you, too. Be a good girl and remember to speak to Mrs. Eze if you need anything at all. She will let us know your needs. You still have her details with you, don't you?" he asked.

"Yes, I do," Adaugo replied, bringing out a piece of paper to show him that she had the information.

"Okay, good girl. Go into your hostel then and get registered. I will be here until you go in," said her father.

And with all the strength and bravery a ten-year-old could muster when being left alone for the very first time, Adaugo walked into the hostel.

CHAPTER SIX

PULLING HER SUITCASE behind her, Adaugo moved quietly down the hallway of her hostel. The floor had some holes in it and she maneuvered and swerved as needed to avoid the wheels of the suitcase falling into the holes. Finally she arrived at room 4B, the designated room which was written on the card handed to her by the matron she had met at registration. Double-checking that the sign on the door to the room matched the number recorded on the card, she took a deep breath and lifted the suitcase into the room.

As she entered, she was greeted by the scent of new wood and cartons. Out of the corner of her eye, she saw a group of six girls already in the room, and she waved to them shyly. Only one of the six girls waved back, the others were lost in a deep discussion and carried on as if they hadn't seen her.

She found her locker, number 112, and set her things in front of it. Looking at the row of lockers, she saw that there were other new lockers, like hers, but these were bolted while hers was not.

Thank God Mum packed those padlocks for me, she thought.

Seeing that there was nothing else for her to do besides unpack her things, given that the only girls she saw seemed oblivious of her presence, she proceeded to open her suitcase on the floor close to her locker. She knelt beside it and removed a stack of old newspapers which she had packed to use as a layer just above the surface of the locker, and then folded her outfits onto the first of three layers she created with the paper. When she was finished unpacking her clothing, she proceeded to arrange her provisions: a packet of Nasco cornflakes, a tin of Dano powdered milk, one box of St. Louis sugar, a sachet of Golden Morn, and a container of Just Juice.

As she brought out the juice, her mind wandered back to Lagos and with this distraction, the conversation from the group of girls seemed to die down, or at least move farther into the distance. She wondered if her father had made it back home and she was overcome with homesickness. She tried hard to fight back the tears, to remain strong, but her stalwart bravery from earlier in the day had escaped and a few drops fell from her eyes onto her bedding. She quickly wiped her eyes and went on to unpack her cosmetics, which she arranged on the first layer of her locker.

While she was finishing this off, she noticed a pair of legs standing beside her. Following the pair of legs upwards, her eyes met those of a girl who she quickly recognised as the one that waved back at her earlier. Adaugo looked across to find that the other five girls were no longer there. *Perhaps they have gone to continue their discussion elsewhere*, she thought.

"Hi, I am Oluchukwu, but you can call me Oluchi," the girl said with a smile and wave of her hand.

"Hi, I am Adaugo."

"Are you also in JSS1?"

"Yes, I am."

"What arm are you?"

"JSS1D, and you?"

"JSS1C. Do you live in Port Harcourt?" Oluchi asked.

"No, I have come in from Lagos," replied Adaugo.

"Me too. In what part of Lagos do you live?" asked Oluchi.

"Mushin, close to Isolo," said Adaugo.

"I know where that is. This is great, we are both Lagos sisters! Come, let me help you make your bed and I will show you around," Oluchi said.

Adaugo hurriedly unpacked the rest of her belongings while Oluchi made her bed and showed her how to stow her empty suitcase. Before they both left the room, she made sure she locked her locker and put the keys in her black waist pouch.

CHAPTER SEVEN

D URING THE WEEKS that followed, Adaugo and Oluchi became inseparable. They went everywhere together and their friendship was very easy. Because they were both from Lagos, they discovered they had many experiences in common and often discussed their homes. During night prep, a time when students were meant to study right after dinner, they would sneak out of the study room to go and get some biscuits to nibble on while they studied.

Most times, Adaugo would pay for their treats, which she did not mind doing because Oluchi had a habit of always forgetting to bring her pouch from class and always promised to pay her back. Besides, Oluchi was her Lagos sister, so it didn't matter. Before long, other classmates even started to call them "the Lagos sisters" and neither of them minded. She was having a good time and she quite liked being in secondary school.

She wrote her first term exams and as expected, did very well.

The weeks passed quickly and before long, there was one week left until the end of first term. Adaugo was thrilled that she would soon be going home. As much as she liked secondary school, she could not wait to eat her mother's *ofe akwu* and rice.

On the night before the students were to vacate for the first term, Adaugo went to bed very early. She was tired from the day, having spent a lot of energy packing, and knew that the following day of travel would be easier if she were well-rested. Arrangements had already been made by her parents for her to fly back to Lagos: Mrs. Eze would come at 7:00am to pick her up from her hostel and take her to the airport where she would get on the 11:15am flight and arrive at Muritala Mohammed Airport Ikeja at noon; her parents would be waiting to take her home.

She was excited to go back home and her last thoughts as she drifted off to sleep were, *by this time tomorrow, I will be at home, in my own bed.*

About three hours after turning in, she felt herself wake up. She wondered why she was awake and decided to use the opportunity to go to the toilet. As she made her way through the door, she heard the distinct voice of Oluchi, amongst other voices, coming from the next room.

What is Oluchi doing awake at this time?

Herself urged her to move closer to the door quietly, the direction from which the voices were coming.

"That Adaugo girl is really stupid *o*," she heard Oluchi say.

"Why do you say so? I thought she was your Lagos sister and you two are very close," one of the other voices said.

"Very close *ke*, she is deceiving herself, I am not close to her *o*. I am just spending her money. The stupid girl has been footing all my break and night prep time meals and she doesn't even complain. All I need to tell her is that I forgot my purse in class and she just pays. I haven't even spent any of my pocket money on snacks. She is my personal bank," Oluchi laughed. "Maybe next term I will not even come with any money because my trusting bank manager will continue to foot my bills, all because she thinks I am her Lagos sister. I don't even care about all her stories about what she wants to be when she grows up. She talks too much and she thinks she is the only intelligent person in the world just because she passed her tests and the teachers like her."

"But this is not fair *o*, Oluchi. So you mean you have been spending this girl's money intentionally?" another girl said.

"Yes *naaa*, did I force her?" Oluchi said.

Adaugo felt like her heart was going to fall through her body and down to her bare feet. She could not believe what she had just heard. Tears filled her eyes as she tried to make sure those hurtful words were coming from Oluchi. She opened the door slightly and peeped and sure enough, Oluchi was there and still speaking. She felt utterly betrayed by this revelation. As she picked up her slippers and walked out of her room into the toilet, the feeling of emptiness grew and she felt confused. Her friend and Lagos sister had turned out not to be her friend but a conniving and calculating girl who was only interested in spending her money.

As she used the toilet, she felt a knot rise to her throat and hot tears filled her eyes. After easing herself, she walked back into her room and climbed back to the top part of her bunk and heard Herself speak:

"Do not be so quick to trust people who are very eager to form associations with you by using common experiences."

She pondered on this but felt too disturbed to go back to sleep. If this was how the world was, she had a lot to learn.

CHAPTER EIGHT

O N THE FLIGHT back to Lagos, Adaugo could not get her mind off what she had heard the night before. The betrayal of trust she had experienced was incomprehensible, especially given that she had been a victim of this calculated betrayal for three months. The lengths Oluchi had gone to in order to pretend she was a friend of Adaugo were extreme; Oluchi had even gone so far as to give her congratulations and encouragement for doing so well in her studies. And yet, even in her betrayal, Adaugo felt gratitude that she had been awakened in time to hear Oluchi's words, so that she would know the truth about this person who had pretended to be her friend. Without having awakened the previous night, the deception would have continued indefinitely.

She was exhausted by the experience and the white noise of the plane lulled her into sleep. She fell into a deep sleep quickly and in it, she dreamed. In her dream, she and Herself sat in a green field similar to one of the fields at her secondary school. Herself sat beside her. Adaugo noticed Herself looked very much like her and mirrored the same emotions she was feeling. Adaugo touched her face and Herself followed with the same gesture. As they both sat there looking across the field, she felt her grief welling up again. It was all too much for her young heart to fathom. Had she not been a good friend to Oluchi? Why had Oluchi spoken such cruel words? As she started to cry, Herself held her hands and began to speak.

"I know you feel really bad about what I showed you, but I thought it was better you saw your friend for who she truly was before she got the chance to inflict more damage on you. I am going to teach you a few things about the world, things I know you are better off knowing and keeping in mind. You are still young. The things I will show you will guide you on whatever path you choose in life."

Adaugo looked at Herself and nodded; Herself then continued to speak.

"The first thing you must remember is that, as difficult as this betrayal feels now, you will heal from it. But you must allow it to leave your heart. Stop lingering over what others did to you. For a heart to heal, you must first remove the dagger.

"As you grow older, you are going to have friends and people you will trust more than others. These people are your inner circle. You will interact with them, spend time with them, share secrets, hopes, dreams, laughter, stories and even tears and disappointment with them. You need to be wise when choosing this inner circle of people because they have the potential to make or mar you.

"If your inner circle is made up of people who constantly and without fail, sit around and engage in idle chat and gossip while arguing about non-issues, before long you will find yourself doing the same.

"On the other hand, if your inner circle is made up of people who are focused, driven and sober-minded, you too will have no choice but to be like them.

"Remember the Bible passage that your father read on the morning you left Lagos for secondary school. I believe it was from Proverbs 13:20.

> 'He that walketh with wise men shall be wise but a companion of fools shall be destroyed.'

"Do you remember?"

"Yes, I do," Adaugo replied.

Herself continued, "I like to believe that there are five different kinds of friends."

"Five categories?"

"Yes, indeed, five categories. They are, Refreshers, Refiners, Reflectors, Reducers and Rejecters. Hold on, I will explain each to you shortly.

"*Refreshers* are friends or acquaintances who strengthen your faith, encourage, energize and motivate you towards achieving your goals and vision. They too have big dreams and share a similar vision with you. When you interact with these people, your energy level goes up and you stay inspired. You will meet only a handful of refreshers in your lifetime and it would be wise for you to identify them quickly and keep in close contact with them as they are good for you.

"Next, *Refiners* are people who help clarify your vision. After interacting with a Refiner, you leave the room feeling more energised and with a clearer definition of your vision. They are very similar to the refreshers.

"The next category of friends are the *Reflectors*. This

group of people neither add to nor subtract from you. They only mirror your energy. You have a great time interacting with them, but you do not feel you have learned anything new, neither do you feel worse off. Most of your schoolmates and perhaps work colleagues in the future will fall into this category."

Adaugo shifted in her seat uneasily as the flight attendant came to ask her if she needed anything. She politely declined any assistance and the beautiful woman smiled at her and went on to attend to other passengers.

As she drifted back to sleep, Herself continued speaking to her.

"The next category of people are called *Reducers*. These are people who actively or unconsciously try to diminish your goals and efforts to bring you down to their comfort level. Most of the time they are people that are too afraid to see beyond their present situation and they get uncomfortable when they see someone with a large vision. You find out that, after interacting with such people for a long period of time, you feel like your energy levels are down.

"Perhaps you may feel some dismay after a long period of interacting with these individuals.

"This leads us to the last category of individuals you will meet. I call them *Rejecters*. These are people who do not understand you or what you are trying to achieve. They keep criticizing everything and do not attempt to understand. After interacting with a rejecter, you may feel a sense of discomfort and lack of peace."

"So what category do you think Oluchi falls under?" Adaugo asked.

"I must leave it to you to draw your own conclusions

regarding that," Herself said.

Adaugo woke up from her slumber in time for her flight to come to a standstill at the Murtala Mohammed Airport runway, but though she was now fully awake, she could not help thinking of her dream and wondering at its validity.

CHAPTER NINE

ADAUGO'S HOLIDAY HAD been very enjoyable and before she knew it, two weeks of it had already elapsed. She had enjoyed eating all of the many foods she had missed when she was away at school, such as *eba* and *egusi* soup, rice and *ofe akwu*. She felt like she was getting heavier, but she did not let this bother her. After all, in two weeks' time she would be returning to boarding school where she would very quickly lose all the weight. Life in boarding school was not easy. She had to fend for herself and walked every day to one of the communal taps to fetch water in her plastic bucket and then walk back to the hostel carrying this in her hand. When she would wake up the following day to have her bath, she would discover that almost half of the water had been stolen by senior students who did not have water.

The food that was served was not the most nutritious and it lacked flavour. The *egusi* soup served in the dining hall, for example, was usually very watery and it was not unusual to find the palm oil floating separately from the rest of the soup. Her mother's cooking while on holiday had been a welcome reprieve from the dining hall's fare.

Adaugo had started to become conscious of her

weight when she realized that any weight gain meant she would need to go to Iya Seyi to have new, larger-sized outfits made. This would mean incurring additional expense for her parents, something she did not want to do. Recently she had heard her dad complain to her mother regarding how little money he had left when Ngozi asked for money to put petrol in her car.

In traditional *Igbo* families, the husband was still expected to provide money for most household expenses, even if his wife had a job. This philosophy is demonstrated in a popular *Igbo* saying, "Mine is mine, and yours is ours." Most men were very happy to take on this responsibility and this was evident in the pet names men used, and still use, for their wives, such as *Oriaku*, translated as 'spender of my money'. Men use such pet names to show off how well taken care of their wives are and it is an exhibition of pride for a man to use such a name for his wife.

Even when disagreements arose in town meetings, men were so quick to insult a man using how shabbily-dressed his wife was as a reference point. Insults such as, "Look at your wife, you can't even take care of her and you call yourself a man," cut to the bone.

Women were happy to be taken care of and usually only chipped in financially when the situation demanded it, such as when a husband was low on cash. When this happened, the husbands were usually pleasantly surprised by their *Oraikus'* ability to provide.

In the exchange over petrol money overheard by Adaugo, Ngozi quietly took out her brown leather purse and took out money to fuel her car to work, but not before offering her husband some money just in case he needed it.

This elicited a smile from Obiora, who responded, "*Oriaku m*, let me know how much you spend on the petrol and I will pay it into your account, *inugo*?"

Ngozi replied, "*Nsogbu adiro, daalu ezigbo di m*, no problem my good husband."

Chapter Ten

O N A SATURDAY morning, Adaugo was awakened by the sound of their neighbour's, Aunty Yemisi's, rooster. Aunty Yemisi had recently decided to dabble in the activity of rearing chickens, though Adaugo was not sure if their neighbour bought the five birds as pets or as a serious business.

The evening before, when she had gone to take in her school day wears and uniforms that had been washed that morning in readiness for going back to school, she noticed the large brown cage with a metal gauze. Out of curiosity, she cautiously peered through the net, wary of the fact that it could be a dog. She did not like dogs as their barks scared her immensely. Allowing her eyes a moment to focus on the darkness within the cage, she noticed some sandpaper-like, wooden chippings on the floor of one of the six compartments of the cage. She remembered that she had seen something similar in one of the matron's houses back in her secondary school.

At least it is not a dog, she thought. She peered closer and with growing confidence and saw a white chicken pacing about the cage, perhaps wondering what her latest visitor was up to. Adaugo noticed a container, like a metal funnel, which contained what she assumed to be food and some water. She peered into the other three compartments and saw white chickens in each one. The fifth compartment housed a red and black rooster who rose up with great pride and cockiness to meet her gaze. She quickly moved to the sixth compartment and noticed it was empty. *That's a bit odd*, she thought.

At that point, she decided to hurry along before her mother began to wonder where she was, and she packed up her school outfits. As she hurried past the cage, she noticed that it was situated right under their room, albeit three floors down. This morning as she awoke, she knew quite well who was responsible for that loud crow. It was that proud red rooster. She tried to block out the sound, but it wouldn't stop.

Cookoro cooo, the roster continued, oblivious to whatever commotion it was causing for the residents and neighbours of the house. Finally, Adaugo decided it was futile to continue trying to go back to sleep. Soon her mother would wake them all for their Saturday chores anyway.

She moved Obioma slightly and slid out of the double bunk bed, and made her way down to the ground using the ladder attached to the end of the bed, being careful of the ceiling fan which moved slowly just above her head. She finally made her way down to the floor of the room and walked past Obiageri, who was still sleeping. She opened the net door and went into the kitchen to the area where the brooms were kept behind the deep freezer.

She made her way into the sitting room and started to sweep the floors. When she was done sweeping the floors, wiped the coffee-brown arms of the chair with a cloth she got from the kitchen. As she bent down to pick up the dirt she had swept out of the room, her mother came out of her room looking puzzled.

"*Gini na-aku?* What is the time?" Ngozi asked, her eyes adjusting to the bright light of the sitting room which was a contrast to the dark room she had just walked out of.

"6 o'clock," Adaugo answered.

"Okay, go and wake the rest, let us pray," Ngozi said.

Adaugo woke her sister, brother and Obiageri and the family gathered together in the sitting room for their morning prayers.

That evening, Adaugo felt a little hungry and asked her mother for some money to buy cobs of corn from Mama Nkechi, the corn seller across the road. Ngozi considered the idea for a while and eventually caved and asked her to bring her purse, from which she pulled out two green 20 naira notes and one 10 naira note.

"Buy two small corn cobs for 10 naira and four big ones for 40 naira, which makes it six corn cobs you would come back with. Make sure they don't give you burnt ones or the ones that are not well roasted. Also make sure they don't cheat you *o*," Ngozi said.

"Yes, Mummy," Adaugo answered.

As she began to unlock the burglar-proof gate which housed the wooden door of their flat, she heard her mum shout, "Do not run on the road and don't talk to anyone. Just buy the corn and come straight home... And watch out for cars!"

"Yes, Mummy," Adaugo answered again. She went to Mama Nkechi's stall and bought the cobs of corn as instructed.

On her way back, she cast her mind back to just before she started in secondary school, to a time when she accompanied her mother to the *Ijora* market in Lagos. Her mother had gone there to buy food stuff in bulk to store in the freezer. While in the market, her mum had passed a woman selling large raw cobs of corn in large baskets. Each basket must have contained at least two hundred cobs of corn.

Her mother had asked, "How much for a basket?"

"400 naira, madam," the corn seller replied.

"How much last?" Ngozi had asked.

"*Oya* take am for 300 naira, Okay pay 300 naira," the woman replied.

"I *dey* come, I will be back," Ngozi replied and walked off holding Adaugo's hand.

It wasn't until years later that the customs of the marketplace on display that day became clear to Adaugo. In truth, Ngozi had no plans at all to buy the corn; she simply wanted to haggle the price to see how much it would actually cost. It was a regular practice for people selling in the markets to inflate their initial prices, knowing that buyers would haggle the price down for their goods. Haggling the price of goods was expected, and sellers accommodated for this by quoting higher prices to begin with.

"Mummy, won't you buy the basket of corn?" she had asked.

Ngozi laughed and replied, "*Biko*, please where would I keep it? I was just checking the price."

Opening the gate of her house, Adaugo did a quick calculation in her eleven-year-old head. *If a basket of corn which contained at least two hundred cobs costs 300 naira, then this means each cob should cost about 1.50 naira. So why did Mama Nkechi sell one little one at 10 naira?*

Herself answered, "Because she has added value to it; she bought charcoal, kerosene and has been fanning the coals all afternoon to produce these roasted cobs you are holding now. She also bought the black nylon bag and newspapers she used to wrap the roasted cobs in so they don't go cold. So you are paying extra for all the extras."

Adaugo marvelled at this as Herself continued. "In this life, if you take something in its raw, perhaps less appealing form, and make some slight changes to it in such a way that it serves a purpose, a need, people will always patronise you and you will make money. Remember when you used to make those piggy banks and books to sell your Uncle Nkem? It is the exact same thing. Always seek to add value and you will never go hungry."

"Amazing…" she thought and pressed the doorbell to her family flat.

CHAPTER ELEVEN

TWO YEARS LATER, Adaugo was now in JSS3 and getting ready to sit for her Junior Secondary School Certificate Examinations. Usually students in their third year of secondary school sat for this examination and passing it was the only way to get into senior secondary school. At this point in secondary school, students offered at least twelve subjects and needed to be tested on their understanding of all the courses. Failure to score more than 50% in any of the subject meant a re-sit if the course was not one of the core subjects, which were Mathematics, English, Integrated Science, Economics, Government and English Literature for intending Art students. No one wanted to be put through the humiliation of re-sitting the exams during summer, not to talk of repeating a class which was the lot of anyone who failed a core subject. Repeating a class usually meant taking the year all over again with students who came in after you. This meant that if you were one of those "sisters" - as older students who were also junior school were called - who was wicked and intolerant to junior students, you would face a lot of humiliation as it would be the perfect opportunity for the juniors to treat you as you had been treating them, and perhaps even worse.

This fear of failure and its impending social consequence caused many of the JSS3 students to go to extra lengths to make sure they passed into senior secondary school.

An additional perk of being a senior was that you were finally allowed to grow your hair. This was a privilege that most junior secondary school students in Adaugo's school craved as they looked longingly at the long and sometimes flowing hair of senior students.

The short haircut of junior students made it very easy for them to be identified among a lot of students. Sometimes senior students intent on proving their seniority would spot JSS3 students who, in anticipation of when they would finally start plaiting their hair, would pass a pen through the bushy hair of these JSS3 students and if the pen did not immediately fall off, the JSS3 students were sentenced to a punishment of frog jumps for at least thirty minutes.

This was a much milder punishment compared to those doled out by matrons if the JSS3 students were caught with bushy hair. Very common punishments included cutting a large portion of grass with nothing but a blunt cutlass, kneeling down for at least an hour on the hard concrete floor or, the very worst, a sentence to go and shave off the entire head of hair.

Adaugo was inclined to thread the very fine line of keeping her hair long enough so as to let a pen go in, but not too long such that if she made a sudden movement of her head, the pen would not fly off. This kept her out of too much trouble in addition to the fact that she also had the ready excuse that she was a Lagos-based student and was waiting for the holidays to come so that she could cut her hair at one of her trusted barbers, because she was scared of head lice.

No one could quite argue with this logic, which was ridiculous on its own as junior students usually shared combs. If there were any head-lice to be caught, they were probably already well settled in her hair.

No one was asking, so she was not telling.

On one Saturday evening, Adaugo was on her way back to class and the constant studying was already showing on her as her daywear was getting quite loose. She had developed a headache the day before and it did not seem to be going away even after sleeping. At this point she decided to go to the school dispensary which was a glorified first aid box with four rooms of beds. The last thing she wanted was to have to lie on the bed.

She did a quick check of her symptoms to make sure it was not malaria. Her mouth was not bitter, her joints did not ache and her urine was colourless, not bright yellow. No malaria, she decided.

She walked through the fields, past her dormitory and climbed the makeshift staircase made of three bricks stacked on top of each other and walked through the non-existent door into the dispensary. As she walked inside, she look around and met no one.

That's odd, she thought.

"Good afternoon," she called out. There was still no answer.

She walked past the consultation room which held a brown desk and two chairs on opposite sides. On top of the brown desk sat a blood pressure testing device which she had seen the nurses on TV use. She had wondered at one point what it would feel like to have the nurse take her blood pressure, but then quickly dismissed the curiosity because, most times, at least on the TV shows she watched, the patients were given the verdict that they had high blood pressure and she wasn't interested in hearing this bad news for herself.

As she carried on walking through the building, she noticed the empty beds. She finally decided the building was empty after she reached the last room and slowly made her way back to the entrance. Deciding there was no point in going back to her hostel only to come back again later, she decided to sit on one of the two wooden, brown benches to wait for the nurse.

After about an hour, she had started to doze off when she spotted someone in a white uniform walking towards the building. She stretched and stood while waiting for the nurse to slowly make her way into the dispensary.

When the woman finally got to the dispensary, Adaugo greeted her politely and told her why she had come.

The nurse frowned and replied with a perfunctory, "Come in."

After listening to Adaugo's complaints, the nurse tossed a white, colourless sleeve filled with ten round tablets of paracetamol at her with the instructions, "Take two tablets in the morning, two in the afternoon and two at night."

Adaugo could feel her blood boiling at the nurse's less than sympathetic response, especially as she was not at her duty post for the past one hour.

"You can go now, what are you still sitting here for?

Come on, run along to your hostel and stop disturbing me," the nurse said.

At this point, Adaugo could feel the sharp response forming on the tip of her tongue but before she could open her mouth to give the rude nurse a little piece of her 13-year-old mind, she heard Herself whisper the following words: "Do not lose your head, just pick up the medicine, thank her and walk away."

Adaugo struggled briefly with Herself and then finally yielded and followed Herself's advice, picked up the tablets and left after thanking the nurse.

As she walked back to her hostel, hot tears of frustration welled in her eyes. She couldn't believe that the woman had very little empathy in a job that required a lot of empathy.

Surely she should not be a nurse, Adaugo thought.

She heard Herself speak again. "Do you want to get yourself worked up because of someone who is clearly unhappy and allow this to ruin your day as a result?"

As she let these thoughts run through her mind, she found herself getting calmer and slightly happier. Then she remembered how, back home, when she used to get angry at her sister, her father would say the same words, "Adaugo, do not lose your head."

At this point, her mood had fully changed from being upset to being very amused. Looking at her black rubber wristwatch, she saw that the time was 5:30pm, only thirty minutes until dinner time.

Time for food, she thought as she pulled out her water bottle from her back pack, swallowed two tablets and hurried along to the school dining hall.

59

PART TWO

Chapter Twelve

ADAUGO SAT IN the passenger seat of a brown 2002 Mazda en route to University. Having passed her Joint Admissions Matriculation Board examinations, she was enjoying her first year as a computer engineering student at the University of Lagos in Lagos, Nigeria. By her side, in the driver's seat, was Wale, a young man she had met on her very first day of university.

Adaugo and Wale had met quite coincidentally. On her first day of University, Adaugo stood in the department office filling in her registration forms. Wale walked up to her and asked if he could borrow her pen when she had finished using it. She had been slightly annoyed by the request since it meant someone was waiting on her and this stranger had taken away from her the luxury of filling out the forms at her leisure, at a pace that suited her.

"No problem," she had replied, dismissively, without looking up. "I will let you use it when I am done."

"Just so you know, I don't plan on stealing your pen, I simply forgot to bring my own," Wale had clarified.

His response caused her to look up at and when she did, she saw a slim, tall guy. Handsome is not how she would have described him, though he also wasn't un-handsome. The shade of his skin reminded her of delicious, lightly-roasted peanuts and his eyes were a beautiful and piercing dark brown. He was wearing a dark blue, chequered shirt tucked into a black, well-fitted pair of chinos trousers held together by a black belt. On his feet were black, immaculately polished shoes and to Adaugo, he looked more like someone going to work rather than one registering for a university programme. There was also an air and confidence surrounding him that was attractive; something in the way he carried himself stated that he was a person who had his life all planned out.

"I'm Wale," he said. "Are you also in computer engineering?"

You think? Adaugo thought it, but hoped she hadn't said such sarcastic words aloud. She looked at him again and decided she hadn't because he was still there, smiling.

She returned the smile and replied, "I am Adaugo, nice to meet you. And yes, I am registering for computer engineering. Sorry if I was rude earlier, about the pen. It's just that in the past two days I have lost two pens and I can't seem to recognise the people I lend them to, and they don't bother returning them. It's highly annoying."

"Don't worry about it, I know exactly how you feel. I too am pen-less, for the same reason!" Wale replied as he took in the sight of the pretty girl in front of him. He placed her height at 5-foot-9-inches or 10-inches, which made her taller than most girls he knew. She had a round and attractive face with lips that looked like they were made for kissing. She was wearing very little makeup and her hair was braided and packed in a ponytail. She was not skinny, neither was she fat, and she had a small waist which separated her slightly slimmer upper body from her curvy hips and long legs. Her skin was the shade of chocolate and she was wearing a white top with flowers at the front and blue jeans. She was a beautiful girl.

The way Wale pronounced "pen-less" in his slight *Yoruba* accent made her chuckle naughtily to herself as it reminded her of a different, very unrelated word.

They shook hands and she carried on filling in her forms, aware that he was watching her intently. This made her palms sweat a little, but she managed to keep her cool regardless. Soon her forms were complete and when she was done, she handed the pen to Wale and stood beside him, arms crossed over her ample bosom.

"Won't you go ahead and submit your forms?" Wale asked.

"I think I will just wait for my pen, thanks," Adaugo responded.

"Alright then," he said. "Nice perfume, by the way."

Adaugo started to protest that she was not wearing any perfume and that it was just her deodorant spray, but quickly thought better of it and responded instead, "Thank you."

When Wale was done, they both went to the queue and struck up a friendly conversation as they waited. It was then she learned Wale also lived in Mushin and had a car and would be happy to give her a ride to and from University every day.

What are the odds, she thought as she sat in the car watching through the corner of her eyes as Wale shifted the gears of the car. She pulled herself away from watching his long, delicate fingers and turned instead to watch the road. In front of their vehicle was a black and brown truck with the following words written on it in red paint:

> *"If you are not a better person tomorrow than you are today, what need have you for a tomorrow?"* – *Rebbe Nachman of Breslov.*

She pondered over these words as the truck noisily veered onto the adjacent road, to the right.

CHAPTER THIRTEEN

A S THEY ARRIVED at the gate leading into the university, their car was stopped by the guard manning the gate. He was a middle-aged man in a fully-starched, brown, short-sleeved shirt and equally starched black trousers.

"Good morning, sir," the guard said to Wale. That he had greeted Wale without so much as a glance at Adaugo was nothing that bothered her. She smiled at the guard anyway, accustomed to not being acknowledged when there was a man in the car.

"Good morning, boss! How's work?" Wale replied. The smile he gave the man fully masked the impatience he felt at the delay being caused by this polite, early morning chit chat.

"We *dey o*, we just *dey* manage. We are managing," the security man replied with anticipation on his face.

"On our way out, I will give you something," Wale said, in essence promising a tip to the security man.

The security man forced a smile that suggested that he did not quite believe Wale's promise and handed him a plastic, rectangular disk on which the following words were written:

CHIKAMSO C. EFOBI

University of Lagos
Car Park
Number 007

After driving around the campus, they were lucky enough to find a parking space in the parking lot close to Moremi Hall, a female hostel which was well known for housing 'girls of substance', a term which signified glorified prostitutes, girls who traded sexual favours for a bit of cash to fund their glamorous lifestyles. Thankfully the space was big enough for Wale to fit the vehicle into while still allowing enough room for Adaugo to open her car door and maneuver her hips out of the cramped space without scratching the black, spotless Jeep parked next to them.

"Are you able to come out?" Wale asked while picking up his house keys, wallet and flash drive from the black dashboard.

"Yes, I can manage," Adaugo called back.

They walked past the boys' hostel amidst cat calls from male students who seemed to appreciate the sight of a pretty girl in a blue and white, fitted cotton top. The girl, like Adaugo, was curvy and pretty, but she was unaccompanied by a man as she walked. So, in the minds of the boys in the hotel, she was fair game. The pretty girl did not seem to mind and wriggled her hips even more, to the delight of the men who were quite entertained by the show she was putting on. They started to clap and she turned and gave them a brief smile before picking up her phone to take a call.

Adaugo and Wale were also amused by the drama and chuckled about it as they walked into their lecture theatre.

When they got inside, Adaugo quickly spotted a pair of seats in the middle row and pointed them out to Wale who agreed they should take them. With thirty minutes to spare before the start of their lecture, Wale brought out his lecture notes to refresh his memory on what was discussed during the last lecture. He did this with a slight furrow on his brow. Adaugo also brought out her book and attempted to study for a few minutes. Ten minutes later, they were both finished preparing for the next lecture and so they sat in silence while watching the rest of their classmates walk in and take a seat.

A short, light-skinned girl walked in and Adaugo studied her closely. She was very pretty and had a cheerful air about her.

"I don't like that girl," Wale said.

"Why?" Adaugo asked, surprised.

"Nothing, I just don't like her. She strikes me as a bad girl," Wale replied.

"How come? Did she do anything to you?" Adaugo was now fully puzzled and curious to find out the reason behind Wale's sudden remark. Looking at the girl in red, she noticed nothing which would suggest that she was either a bad or unlikeable person. In fact, she quite liked how cheerful this girl seemed as she greeted a number of people before finally settling beside one of her friends. She also smiled at Adaugo, and Adaugo smiled back.

"I just don't like her," Wale repeated.

"Well, that's a shame because she is my cousin from my mother's side."

Wale spun around sharply to his right to meet Adaugo's serious, yet blank gaze.

"Are you serious? Is she really your cousin?" Wale

asked.

"Yes, she is and I take offense at what you have just said about my cousin. It is not fair, especially as she has done nothing to you," Adaugo replied, still with a straight face.

"Oh my God. I am so sorry. I never knew she was your cousin. Please forgive me," Wale said, looking quite flustered and remorseful. Adaugo was not sure if what she saw on his forehead was sweat or if her eyes were deceiving her.

"Well, does this mean you now like her and she no longer strikes you as a bad girl?" she asked, looking quite defiant.

"Yes, indeed! She is your cousin, so she is a good girl. I never knew she was your cousin, honestly, or I would not have said it," Wale said with desperation in his voice.

"Well…she isn't," Adaugo replied with a smile.

"Are you serious? She is not your cousin?" Wale looked quite relieved now.

"No, she isn't, but you need to be careful about what you say about people you don't know because you never know, you may be speaking to her cousin or her friend," Adaugo replied.

"Oh. Yes, I agree; lesson learned," Wale replied. Their Engineering Maths lecturer walked in then with a stack of lecture notes and placed them on the lectern located at the front of the theatre.

As the lecturer began to introduce the topic for the day, Adaugo heard Herself say, "Never say anything about someone which, if called to testify, you are unable to repeat to the person's hearing or the hearing of the person's close friend. This will save you a lot of trouble in life."

"Yes, indeed," Adaugo agreed under her breath.

Chapter Fourteen

IN HER SECOND year of university, Adaugo lived in one of the female hostels on campus, called Madam Tinubu Hall, or MTH for short. It was a massive, three-story building that spanned seven blocks. Each floor of a block had twenty rooms, ten on each side. Her room number was D302 which meant that she lived in the second room on the third floor of the D block of the hostel. In essence, MTH was an expansive block of flats.

The flats had double bunk beds, just like in her secondary school and, as usual, she stayed on the upper bunk. She had come to accept her fate of always staying on the top bunk and was very used to jumping up and down from her bed to the floor anytime she needed something from her massive locker. The lockers there were quite different from those in her secondary school days because this time she could hang her outfits on hangers rather than having to fold them, like she did during her days in Rivers state.

MTH was situated somewhat at the center point between the university's main gate and the engineering section of campus. On days when the Lagos sun was not blasting heat furiously she would take the twenty minute walk from her room, down the three flights of stairs, over to the pedestrian walk, past the Senate building and into the engineering facility.

Now that she lived in the hostel, she missed the morning and evening car rides with Wale, but she was also thankful that she did not have to bear the painful traffic jam which usually marred their journeys to and from home. She now looked forward to locking eyes with him when they met in class and was always comforted by the fact that even though she did not drive with him, he would still reserve a seat for her where they could catch up on happenings, everything from the Nigerian news to philosophical topics, such as what happens after death.

She found it so easy to speak to him because it seemed like they both had the same questions regarding religion and life after death, and they never seemed to run out of things to talk about. He was a breath of fresh air and they would talk for hours while everyone else physically present around them seemed to fade into the distance.

Adaugo thought about her feelings for Wale and concluded that she was not quite sure if it was love or not, at least she wasn't sure if it was the kind of love she had read about it in the Mills and Boom novels she used to sneakily read in secondary school. Sometimes after night prep she would read them privately, or sometimes she read them within the full view of other students, but always she wrapped her novel in a calendar to avoid being judged by the prudes in her class who could not bear to see the suggestive books covers of these novels without getting overly excited.

She knew she cared for Wale, but it felt more like

closeness with a kindred spirit, someone like her who had also suffered the loss of a sibling and was, as she was, now searching for a truth that satisfied all doubts. Their closeness often brought questions to the mouths of classmates and before long everyone wondered if they were dating. Some of Wale's friends made fun of him regarding his closeness with Adaugo, which he relayed back to her. This usually caused her to laugh out loud in a dismissive manner. They were not dating and as far as she could tell, had no plans to do so if they could help it. There closeness was not a dating relationship; they were simply kindred spirits and wonderful companions.

After classes, Adaugo would return to the hostel with two of her friends, Ivie and Tola. Ivie was from Urhobo in Delta State and Tola was from Lagos, making her a Lagosian, as people who hailed from the commercial capital of Lagos were called.

Both girls were about the same age as Adaugo, although Ivie measured at five-feet-ten-inches, half an inch taller than Adaugo, and never failed to remind Adaugo of this fact. Tola was ten months older than the other two girls and also measured at just above five-feet-nine-inches.

Ivie and Tola were both studying chemical engineering and would walk down from their department, which was located in a different building from the rest of engineering, and wait for Adaugo to finish her lectures. Then the three would walk back to their hostel amidst laughs and banter.

"Hmmm, you like this Wale guy, *shaaa*," Ivie said one afternoon after Adaugo had said good bye to Wale.

"Like who *abeg*?" Adaugo replied, feigning ignorance

at the subject of Ivie's comment.

"Stop pretending, *jor*. You like him," Tola chipped in.

"I know that look. Look at your pupils, they are dilating! This is a sure way to know if someone has feelings for someone else!"

"*Hian*! *Biko*, please how did you get to know that one? Are you speaking from experience?" Adaugo replied with a wink.

"As if I would go about with a mirror in my hand just in case I saw someone I liked so I could quickly check to see if my pupils are dilated, *abi*? *Abeg*, please, I read it on the internet. My Starbuzz modem finally agreed to open a page after thirty minutes of waiting last night, so I saw it there," Ivie replied while tossing some peanuts in her mouth.

"*Nawa* for you *o*… so you did not see anything else to browse at night other than how to recognize the signs of love?" Adaugo said, chuckling.

"*Eh* leave it like that for me. I also saved some Westlife pictures, particularly one of Brian, my husband to be," Ivie replied with a dreamy look in her eyes.

"Keep dreaming, girl. From where to where would you see Brian to marry? *Abeg*, please give me peanuts to eat. You are finishing it!" Tola said, grabbing the bag of peanuts from Ivie.

"Dreams do come true. Watch out, I will marry Brian from Westlife."

"*Anugom*, I have heard," Adaugo replied, not believing this for a second.

Chapter Fifteen

THE NEXT DAY, the three girls left their hostel at 8:00am which was early enough to allow them to get to the lecture theatre on time for their first 9:00am lecture. The lecture was Engineering Mathematics 2, known as GEG201 for short, which was given by a lecturer whom the three girls agreed was rather boring. However, because the course was a compulsory one, they attended, albeit grudgingly.

GEG201 was taken by every engineering student regardless of what department they were in. This meant that the three girls could attend the same lecture, which was a rather rare occurrence. What this also meant was that there were usually very few seats left for anyone who decided to leisurely stroll in fifteen minutes prior to the start of the lecture. By 9:00am, the lecture hall was packed to the rafters and those students who had arrived late were left outside and struggled to hear and see what the lecturer was teaching.

There was usually no electric power supply to the lecture theatre and when there was, it was erratic. Whatever little daylight was available was blocked by the vast number of students struggling to listen while positioned at the door. This also did not bode well for cross-ventilation because there were only two doors, one at the front and one at the back of the theater. The back door was usually bolted shut at night and was hardly ever opened early enough to matter to those who needed to attend early lectures.

With just one door serving the dual purpose of being the source of light and air, the lecture theatre, which had the capacity to hold at least five hundred students, was usually rather hot and dark. Anyone who had the misfortune of standing outside was bombarded by a mixture of the putrid smell of sweat, hot air and the constant smell of rotten eggs as a result of someone farting. This rotten egg smell usually elicited the coordinated response, "Hmm… who did that?" And this was usually followed by the waving of anything across the face, anything at all which could aid in expelling the pungent smell of fart. This usually constituted a distraction because anyone who was already struggling to both hear what the lecturer was saying and write notes, would use the same note to fan himself. This coordinated fanning meant that those stuck outside the lecture theatre were unwilling recipients of this gift of human gas.

At first, Adaugo wondered who the elusive holder of the engineering lecture theatre back door key was, but after attending lectures in the same conditions day after day, she gave up questioning this.

"Hurry up Ivie, we will be late," Tola beckoned.

"I'm on my way, one minute," Ivie responded while taking one last look at herself in the hostel mirror. There was limited mirror space as Adaugo was also trying to squeeze in to see her reflection while applying her pink, absolute lip gloss, something she had purchased from Mama Tope, a woman who hawked items of makeup each evening.

"We are coming *abeg*, no vex. Please don't be angry," Adaugo called out to Tola.

When Ivie and Adaugo were both satisfied that they looked good enough to bless the outside world with their presence, they picked up their bags and jogged along to meet up with Tola, who was already heading down the stairs.

As the trio walked out of their hostel and through the gate, being careful to stay on the concrete floor for fear that their heels would dig into the grass, they were greeted by whistles from Mr. Ajala the photographer. Mr. Ajala had a little kiosk toward the left of MTH gate. From his perch, he chanted and whistled at any reasonably decent-looking female to encourage them to take pictures.

He called out things such as, "Baby, you are looking delicious, are you going for a beauty contest today?" or, "Fine girl, let me give you just one shot, you are looking very take away today." His comments usually earned him only smiles and nods from female students who were in a hurry to meet up with their lectures. For others who were in no such hurry, Mr. Ajala would persuade them with more sweet words until they finally caved in and posed for a 5 x 7 picture, which he then sold to them for 35 naira a shot. At the point when the customer was paying, he would upsell them by encouraging them to pay for a 6 x 9 picture instead, which cost 50 naira.

Mr. Ajala was quite skilled at this and seemed to know the right words to use and who would be most willing to respond positively to his words; he would capitalise on it until they patronised him. He also knew how not to waste time on those who would never patronise him. No one would blame him for being good at his work as he had four children and a wife to support through the income from his photographs.

As they walked passed him, Mr. Ajala called out to them, "Sweet princesses, come, let me give you one professional shot. Oh, you look *superlative* today, and those shoes sister! All the men are going to faint today and the girls will be so envious of the three of you. Honestly, come let me give you a professional shot. In fact, I can give you a free shot!"

The girls felt serenaded and flattered by his praises, so they quickly decided to take a picture. After all, Ivie was wearing new shoes that day.

"Is the picture really free?" Adaugo asked, feeling hopeful at the possibility of having something for nothing.

"Yes sister, one shot is free. I just love how you three look today," Mr. Ajala replied with a coy smile.

"Alright then, where should we stand?" Tola asked.

They posed for the one picture but before long, they began to enjoy the experience and took even more, with Mr. Ajala's voice in the background encouraging them. "Oh beautiful, oh stand this way, hands on your hips, look fierce, brilliant!"

When they were done, they inspected the pictures through his camera lens and decided on ten pictures they would pay for.

As they hurriedly walked off to meet up with their lectures, the photographer counted his earnings and muttered to himself, "350 naira, not bad for a twenty minute job. Mrs. Ajala will be in a good mood, no headache tonight!" He felt a familiar, dull ache between his thighs as he imagined the feel of his wife's thighs matching his rhythm, and her face contorted with the pleasure of lovemaking.

CHAPTER SIXTEEN

ADAUGO RESTED ON her bunk bed and cast her mind back to the day's events. Her roommates were fast asleep and the light from her laptop was the only source of illumination in her dark room. Gloria, one of her roommates, snored and disrupted the otherwise silent room.

She let her thoughts drift; however, the yellow light of her mobile phone briefly interrupted her thoughts. She quickly checked the phone and replied to the message she had received, and then she managed to drift back into her thoughts. She was not sure of what she was thinking about, only that she was thinking of many things. She looked at her table clock, a constant reminder that she was another second older, and she thought of her childhood and the days when there had been fewer cares in the world. Right before Ifeoma died, her biggest problem was how to get her hair plaited by Iya Seyi, who would firmly hold her head in her thighs in a bid to prevent her from making sudden movements and spoiling the emerging cornrows as she tried her best to control Adaugo's wayward and full, dark hair. She smiled at the memories. *Things are certainly different now, definitely different*, she thought as her eyes fell to the pictures she had collected from the photographer.

As she looked closely at the picture, she saw some faces of total strangers in the background and a thought occurred to her. *In how many people's pictures has my face appeared without my knowledge? For how many people has my image served as a background to their pictures?*

She heard Herself speak, "Just as we can be part of someone's picture without even knowing it, we can affect someone's life without realising it. The choices we make every minute of every day can contribute to making someone's life a little bit better or worse even without intending to."

She marveled at the intensity of the words she had just heard Herself speak.

Herself continued, "Little acts of kindness, such as smiling to an attendant at the supermarket, leaving the door open for someone behind you, saying thank you, these don't cost a thing but go a long way towards making people's lives happier. This kind gesture could then cause the attendant to go on to say kind words to other people and then before you know it, you have started a cycle of kindness."

"This is deep," she said to Herself. She determined that perhaps the original person may not have intended to affect so many people but indirectly, he or she had.

She remembered a story that her mother told her about a boy who went out in the rain to distribute Christian tracts against his father's warning. During his rounds that evening, he slipped a tract into the letter box of an old woman who was just about to commit suicide. The woman had been frustrated with living life alone after the death of her husband of over forty years.

Just as the old woman was about to take the poison, the tract came in through her letter box and she read it. The boy didn't know that just by going out to share those tracts, even in the cold rain, he was saving the life of someone and would probably never know it.

CHAPTER SEVENTEEN

A FEW MONTHS later, the university was buzzing with students preparing for second semester examinations. As a second year student, Adaugo felt a bit of *déjà vu* because it reminded her of secondary school days when she used to work so hard to study for examinations. Perhaps the stake was not as high now because failing a course meant carrying over, or re-sitting, the course with students from the next set. Unlike secondary school days, there was no shame in carrying over one or two courses as long as they were not prerequisite courses, those which needed to be passed in order to take the next one in the upper year.

As in the domino effect, if a person failed a prerequisite course it meant the next one in the series could not be taken until the current one had been passed. The implication of failing a prerequisite course was an automatic extra year at university.

However, even with all the pressure and looming risk of an extra year, Adaugo could not bring herself to study for this particular examination. She found herself preferring to surf the internet for nothing in particular. Every time she picked up her intimidating text book, she remembered she needed to either reply to a text message or go to the loo.

This is not going well... At this rate, I will probably fail woefully, she thought. After this realisation, she decided that the best way to wake herself up was to take a power nap. She had read about the effectiveness of these short naps and decided to try it out.

What harm could come of napping for fifteen minutes? I have almost wasted three hours already and achieved nothing, she thought as she dozed off.

She was suddenly awakened by the rustling of her roommates who had just come back from class. In panic and total confusion she shot up from her bed and checked her wristwatch. It was now 11:00pm which meant that her short, fifteen-minute nap had turned into five hours. Wide-eyed, she looked across the room and checked her phone. She had missed five calls and had two messages, one from Ivie and one from Tola, during the time she was asleep and they wanted to know when she planned to join them in class.

Not any time today, she muttered to herself as she sent the following text message to the two girls:

"I slept off, just woke up. I have covered three chapters tonight. Ask me about this when we see each other tomorrow."

After sending the message, she was filled with a new zest for her reading. Perhaps it was the fifteen minutes turned five-hour power nap. Perhaps it was the fact she had just told a white lie which she knew she would be accountable for the next day when she saw Ivie and Tola. She could not quite explain it, but she knew that all she wanted to do now was study.

She put her phone inside her wardrobe and locked it up for safe keeping, packed her books, spread her wrapper around her neck and headed down the stairs towards the hostel reading room. As she avoided the pockets of water that had collected on the damaged floor in front of the reading room, she remembered the Law of Inertia which she learned during her secondary school Integrated Science class: *Every body continues in its state of rest or constant motion until is acted upon by an external force.*

Perhaps this white lie and the potential of being accountable for this lie was the external force she desperately needed to get moving again.

CHAPTER EIGHTEEN

THE FOLLOWING DAY Adaugo was exhausted from staying up so late to study. Even though she had given herself the lofty target of completing three chapters of her textbook, she found that she could hardly understand what she was reading. She looked around at her fellow classmates who were now settling in for the revision lesson and everyone seemed so fulfilled and happy. They certainly did not appear to feel out of place with all the studying and they all seemed like they were having an easier time than her.

Watching her classmates, particularly Omotayo, the daughter of an economics department lecturer, argue with a male classmate about one of the facts she had studied made her wonder if she was blessed with a little less brain capacity than her classmates. She cast her mind back to when studying came naturally to her and longed for those good old days. Now it was very difficult to motivate herself to do any studying. The whole thing was rather boring. Still, she put up a brave face and pulled out her jotter where she had scribbled notes the night before on items she thought she understood.

Seriously, there must be a better way than trying to

understand this stuff, she thought to herself.

She was still lost when Wale approached her from the other side of the class.

"I recognise that frown," he said. "Is CEG 256 still bothering you?"

"Unfortunately, yes," she replied.

"Well, it bothers me too and I have decided that I will just cram the thing and pass. I don't understand it."

"Oh well, what choice do we have? We have to pass, don't we?" Adaugo said with a sigh.

"We sure do... We do, indeed," Wale said, settling into the all too familiar position to her left as the bespectacled lecturer, Mr. Thompson, walked in.

After lecture, Wale walked back with her to her hostel and as they got to the entrance, he put his hand in his satchel, brought out a purple book and handed it her.

"Is that for me? What is it?" Adaugo asked, giving him a suspicious look.

"A book I bought for you. Well, technically not for you as I have read it. I just finished reading it and I feel you should read it too," Wale replied.

"Hmmm... what is it about?" she asked, still suspicious.

"How will you know if you don't read it? Trust me, you will love it. I have to run and try to beat the Ojuelegba traffic."

"Alright then... Thank you," she said as she gave him a hug.

"See you tomorrow, I will call you tonight so you can tell me how you are getting on with the book, okay?"

"No worries, Inspector Gadget. I know you want to make sure I read the book and I won't disappoint."

"I trust you will not," Wale said, winking.

She studied the purple book cover which had a picture of an Asian man in a black suit on the front, as well as the words, *Rich Dad, Poor Dad.*

This should be interesting, she thought to herself as she climbed the stairs.

After having her dinner of rice, *ofada* stew and fried plantain which Tope, the "any work" brought for her, she settled into bed for a quick nap which she felt she badly needed considering that the only sleep she had enjoyed were the three hours she managed to get when she got back from the reading room that morning. As she turned to her left side to face the wall, she cast her mind back to Wale and how his lean, tall body felt on her chest when she hugged him good bye. She knew she was starting to feel something for him but was not sure what. Ivie and Tola certainly never let her rest whenever the subject of boyfriends came up. For some reason, they felt convinced that they were a couple and she was only hiding it and she had since concluded that it was not worth the effort trying to convince them otherwise as they wouldn't listen.

She chuckled as she remembered how he tried to keep a stern face while warning her to make sure she read the book. This would be the first time he recommended something so seriously to her. What was so special about this book? Her thoughts were replaced by a raw fear that she would not do well this semester. She was certainly struggling with at least two of the courses. She wondered whether the answer lay in the purple-covered book. Perhaps this was why Wale was so adamant that she read it. A flood of hope washed over her and she sat up excitedly and jumped down from her bed. She knocked over her unwashed lunch plates as her feet hit the floor. The noise elicited a loud hiss from Monsurat, her other roommate, who was having a nap and felt disturbed by Adaugo's noise.

I wonder why she is so grumpy today, she thought as she grabbed the purple book and climbed back into her bed.

With her back against the wall, the same wall she had been facing only a few minutes before while struggling to sleep, she once again admired the glossy purple book cover.

Well, here goes nothing, she thought as she turned to the first page and started to read.

CHAPTER NINETEEN

WALE GOT HOME that evening and dumped his keys and wallet on his floor close to his twenty-one-inch television, which sat in the right-hand corner of his humble, one bedroom apartment. He had tried to decorate the apartment, which was located close to Idioro market, to the best of his abilities and was proud of his efforts and bragged about this whenever his sisters came to visit him. His comments usually elicited some muffled laughter because although he felt he had done a grand job, his eighteen-year old twin sisters, Taiwo and Kehinde, only saw a dingy looking, coffee-coloured cushion which matched his equally curious looking, coffee-coloured, round centre table with round glass. On top of the centre table sat an oval glass bowl which was meant to hold potpourri. The bowl had held potpourri once as planned, but the dry flowers had lost their scent and the glass bowl had now been turned into a makeshift collecting place for such items such as his keys, cigarette packs his friends left behind, chewing gum and sometimes condoms.

On the right side of the room sat a twenty-one-inch television on a TV stand which, in turn, sat on a brown and coffee-coloured rug which he bought from Mushin market. He always felt he had overpaid for it. To its left, there was a white, miniature refrigerator. At the far left of the room, opposite his door, sat his vitafoam mattress which had white and coffee-coloured beddings on them.

He turned on the television and opened his mini-fridge to see whether there was some stew left from what Lara, his sex buddy, had brought over for him the last time she visited. Even though they got along and had mind blowing encounters which left his head spinning, in recent days he was beginning to feel like the relationship was becoming a bit more than he had intended. He was not sure if she was starting to see him as her boyfriend and he didn't dare ask.

His suspicions began when she started to insist on cooking for him, something she had never done in the six months they had been seeing each other. Theirs had been one of the most casual interactions from the start. She would call to check if he was home and ask if he was interested in some company. He would answer in the affirmative and she would come over, no unnecessary conversations about how lectures went, no dates, no being seen in public. When they were done, she would sleep over, pick up her bags, give him a kiss on his forehead and rush off for her lectures at Federal Technical College Yaba, also in Lagos.

Their arrangement had been perfect and he couldn't quite believe his luck, especially as she was not a bad looking girl and very gifted in the sac. She seemed to be okay with the casual arrangement and referred to him as her friend whenever she received a call from men he was sure were her other boyfriends. She would silently signal for him to turn down his TV, pulling up the bed covers to cover her chest like he had not seen everything over and over again and respond, "Yes Chief, I am not at home, I am in a friend's house. Okay, I will see you tomorrow evening. No problem." The person on the other line seemed not to be sure and she would reassure the caller of her intentions to visit him, end the call and they would resume from where they left off.

He was perfectly comfortable with the arrangement and never asked who the men were, in the same way she did not ask if he had any girlfriends. Theirs was strictly physical; however now, he was not so sure because she was beginning to pester him for dates and had recently asked him to accompany her to a wedding. That was one thing he knew never to do with a girl who he saw no future with – never go to a wedding or any family-themed event with her. He politely declined her proposal with the excuse that he had university work to prepare for.

Lara suspected it was a lie but shrugged it off; after all, they were not dating and he was not obliged to attend events with her.

Wale wished he could feel more than a sexual attraction for Lara because she seemed like a genuinely nice girl, but the space had been filled by someone else whom he had had in his heart for close to three years.

As he thought of Adaugo he felt that familiar warmth in this centre. He could not explain how he had become captivated by a female for this long without the ability to shake it off. He had always prided himself as a ladies' man, but this girl was special. He didn't believe in love at first sight and often laughed at romantic movies which centred on the idea. His sisters on the other hand embraced the idea, and he often made scornful sounds registering his cynicism whenever they came to visit him and put on one of such movies.

Now he wasn't so sure because he had been drawn to her from the first time he saw her from across the hall on that registration day. He wasn't sure what exactly drew him to her. Maybe it was this all knowing aura she exuded, or the way her forehead furrowed as she tried to understand what she was meant to fill in on the form, or how she kept pushing her errant braid out of her face. He knew he just had to speak to her, but hadn't known what to say. It was when, lost in thought, she put her pen in her mouth that he found his opportunity. He quickly hid his own pen in his bag, hid some of the forms he had already filled so she would not spot his deception, and walked up to her. When she looked up in impatience and mild annoyance, he saw the face of one who was used to being bothered by men and could not blame her one bit.

He smiled as he remembered her responses to him in that first meeting. Still looking in the refrigerator, he was pleased to find a little stew in the blue plastic bowl, just enough for one person. As he opened the lid, he discovered there was no meat left in it though. He began to wonder what must have happened to the meat when he remembered he had a midnight snack while revising the night before. He was too tired to warm the stew up and was thankful for the fact that NEPA did not provide electric power that afternoon, which meant that he could not have warmed the stew even if he had wanted to.

He grabbed the remnant of the *agege* bread from his breakfast that morning, and put it against his nose to establish its freshness. *Not too bad*, he decided as he tucked the bread into his makeshift meal.

There was a Nigerian soap opera, *Family Ties*, showing on TV and he settled down to watch it even though he did not follow the programme. A tall, pretty, chocolate skinned girl with rounded hips came into view and he was amused by how much she reminded him of Adaugo. Every female with the slightest physical similarity did these days. He closed his eyes as he reminisced on how much electricity he felt when she hugged him. He had done all he could that afternoon to stop himself from putting his hands on her hips and pulling her closer to himself. All he could think about during the three seconds the hug lasted was the smell of her strawberry body mist. If only he could put his lips on her smooth neck and plant a kiss there.

He closed his eyes as he wondered how she must feel under his touch. How would she look if he ever got the chance to take off her braids from the prison she always subjected them to? He would let the braids fall at the sides on her soft round face and hold her face in his hands as he let his lips finally kiss her.

He was often tempted to do this whenever she put a sweet in her mouth and wished he could swap places with the confection. That would be heaven, pure heaven. Even as his thoughts continued to build up to what would be their first love making session, he was reminded of the fact that he was not sure how she felt about him. If she felt anything other than a platonic friendship, she was doing a good job hiding it. He did not know how much he could go on masking how he felt about her out of fear that she would stop trusting him and interacting as freely as she currently did. The fear of losing her as a friend always stopped him from making the move. The greater fear of screwing it up if she finally accepted and they started dating was much greater and most times kept him from asking her to take the next step with him.

For now, he would continue to make do with their friendship and hoped against hope that he could continue to keep up with the façade.

CHAPTER TWENTY

A DAUGO OPENED THE book given to her by Wale and began to read. At first the concepts seemed fuzzy and complicated, but as she continued to turn the pages, this gave way to a new set of observations. She felt completely engrossed with the possibility that formal education might not be the only path to financial freedom, a concept that is a cornerstone theme of *Rich Dad, Poor Dad*. As she read on, she felt like she had finally eaten the proverbial apple from the tree of wisdom and for the first time ever was able to envision a life in which she could excel.

Prior to reading this book, she had been conditioned to believe that the only way she could be successful was through good grades, graduating with a first class or perhaps a 2:1, applying for jobs, getting a job, working hard and being promoted until her retirement pot was full enough, all of which was a tedious path in Nigeria. Through her reading, she began to accept new definitions of success outside of the path she had been raised to follow.

Retirement in Nigeria was never a sure bet. On a number of occasions on NTA 2 channel 5, Adaugo had watched coverage of frail-looking women and men waiting hopelessly in the sun for someone, anyone, to tell them when they would get paid. Some of these men and women had died while waiting and never received a single payment owed to them for the working years of their youth. She had often wondered why this was so, especially as Nigeria was a very rich country in terms of crude oil and agricultural lands, amongst other national assets. More often than not, she was struck by the intense sadness of these men and women, feeling it deeply herself, even though it was not her anguish to feel. Who was responsible for stopping pension payments? One Sunday, her father finally told her that some wealthy government officials were responsible for this treatment of pensioners.

Through her reading, she was also particularly happy to find a way out of this loop, especially since one of her lecturers had referred to those who were destined to graduate with a second class lower grade (2:2) as "a bunch of failures." With the principles she was learning through reading Wale's book, she was comforted; now she would not be a failure. She would be a business woman. She would excel in business and perhaps employ some people who graduated with 2:1 just to make a point. She and Wale had certainly joked about this in the past and at the time she thought it was a mere wild dream; now, after reading this book, it was no longer just a dream, it was a possibility. It was far-fetched, but possible. All she needed was a very good business idea, something revolutionary that would change the world and make her very rich.

By Saturday of the following weekend, she had

finished the book and had begun to set about thinking of business ideas. But no matter how hard she tried, nothing came to her. She focused on this throughout the rest of that Saturday up until Sunday morning, but her notepad remained blank with the exception of a few doodles written and shaded in blue biro. She was getting frustrated at this point. She wondered why the ideas were not coming to her, and started questioning whether there might be a devil working against her.

Her thoughts were suddenly interrupted by a loud banging on the bedroom door. She was startled by this and jumped out of the bed, hoping it was one of the women who hawked outfits, or Mama Tope. Whoever it was, she hoped to be able to quickly dismiss them in order to return to her ideas generation exercise, though she was beginning to feel like giving up on it. As she moved the metal cylindrical bolt of her light wooden door, she was almost jumped.

"You! Girl, where have you been hiding? I hope you have not been camping any man," Ivie said as she let herself in.

"We have been worried about you. You seem to have disappeared into thin air! No call, no texts, nothing! Are we quarrelling?" echoed Tola.

"No, nothing is wrong girls, I have just been very busy that's all, and as you can see, there is no man in here so get your mind out of the gutter," Adaugo said, gesturing to the otherwise empty room.

"Okay *o*, if you say so," Ivie said as she helped herself to some Pringles Original from Adaugo's locker, without permission. After she opened it, she asked if she could have some. Adaugo answered affirmatively in a non-committal tone and silently pondered why Ivie had felt the need to ask since she had already opened the package.

The three girls chatted for the rest of the evening and even though she had initially been upset about the unwelcome intrusion of her friends, she was thankful because it provided her with something to distract her from the fact that she had not come up with a business idea. After the girls left, Adaugo was left with her thoughts and again began to ponder. It was at this point that she heard Herself speak for the first time in a long while. She had certainly missed their conversations, especially now that she was in a bit of a pickle.

However instead of Herself providing her with the answers she sought, she asked a question. "Adaugo Obi, what is your life purpose?" she asked. "What are you on earth for?"

Adaugo shifted uneasily in her bed because the question had never crossed her mind in that way. She had heard pastors preach this but she always thought it had to do with living the most squeaky clean life, without any sin nor blemish, and after trying so many times to obey the rules, she had given up. Now this question was more personal, it was about her impact on earth given the resources she had available to her, including her mind, her body, her soul and perhaps Herself.

Now she had much more to think about as she put away her notebook.

PART THREE

"He who would be what he ought to be must stop being what he is." [Meister Eckhart]

CHAPTER TWENTY-ONE

THE YEAR WAS 2009 and Adaugo sat in one of the six seats in her shared office at Triumph Bank. She was a Customer Relationship Officer and shared an office with two other staff members, a female named Bola, in her twenties, and Abdul, a corporate banker from Kwara state.

Kwara state is located in Western Nigeria and even though it was predominantly a Yoruba state, it had minorities who spoke Hausa language and bore Muslim names.

Abdul was a good looking man whose love for anything in a skirt knew no bounds, even though he was married to one wife and had two beautiful kids, a boy and a girl. Their picture adorned the screen of his Blackberry phone which was more of an appendage than a phone. He could not stop checking and laughing at his phone and when he was not laughing at something he had just seen on the phone, he was using the office phone to call one of his girlfriends to apologise for not showing up as planned. Adaugo suspected that the the reason he usually didn't show up was because his wife got wind of his plans to stray and nipped it in the bud, surprising him by picking him up from work. Either this or it was because one of his other girlfriends had called him for a visit, whom he had no scruples visiting with in the branch car.

No one could blame him for his activities; he was good looking and he could talk the talk. Of course talking the talk, as far as he was concerned, was generally saved for the ladies and not usually applied to generating more income or meeting his monthly sales target.

Bola, on the other hand, was very quiet. Dark skinned and about five-feet-six inches, she walked with a slight limp. She had graduated from Lagos State Polytechnic, or LASPOTECH as it was called for short, and was a devout Christian. Her title was Direct Sales Representative, a fancy way of saying she was a contracted staff member whose salary was wholly and solely dependent on how many potential customers she was able to convert to real customers. This lack of job security forced her to work tirelessly and diligently every day, even when doing so included cold calling potential customers, or "pipes" as they were referred to, to make sure they were quickly converted to customers. She was not limited on the kind of account she could open, meaning she could bring in a business, personal, or large corporate account into the bank, as long as she was creating accounts. However, large corporate accounts meant big money for her and this was usually the focus of her attention. This desperation also meant she was subjected to all sorts of advances from sleazy, overweight, often married men who saw her as nothing more than a fresh piece of meat to consume.

Bola often shared stories with Adaugo about times when randy men would stop midway during sales presentations to ask her to perform a sexual act. This was usually followed up by a look of sheer surprise when she quite blatantly told them that she was a Christian and had no business doing such things. The men, who were used to other female bankers being more agreeable to their suggestion, were usually shocked by this response and before they could react, Bola would be limping away, out the door.

Adaugo was in charge of the Priority segment, a step above mass market. The minimum opening account balance for a priority account was 1.5 million naira. With the exchange rate of 250 naira to a pound, this was a lot of money to ask a new customer to have before opening an account. She knew it would be a difficult job but at the time she interviewed for the position, she did not think she would get it and if she was perfectly honest with herself, did not want it. Deep down inside, she still nursed a dream of owning her own business, and settling for working for someone else always felt disappointing. However, everyone reminded her that there was no money in the economy and encouraged her to take the first job she got to gain experience.

"Well, I don't know what experience I am gaining here," she thought while waiting for Abdul to finish one of his long phone conversations. She was getting impatient at the whole set up and shared a silent look of irritation and disdain with Bola who, like Adaugo, was also waiting to use the phone.

She pulled out her mobile phone and sent a text to Anozie, her boyfriend, "Abdul is at it again with the phone. I might just scream at him!!!"

She put the phone down and gave Abdul another look of pure menace, willing him to hang up his call, and picked up her mobile phone again just as it beeped. It was a reply from Anozie. "Please take it easy with the guy. Are we still on to meet at Cherries restaurant after work tonight?"

She giggled and replied, "I will try to... yes we are. See you later."

While she waited for Abdul to finish his call, she stared out the window and her mind drifted to the strange occurrence she had experienced the last time she met Anozie at Cherries restaurant. He had been late arriving for their date and called to say how sorry he was for keeping her waiting. The day was fine and a light breeze kept her cool while she waited outside the restaurant, and it occurred to her that it was too beautiful outdoors to wait for Anozie inside. So, she had stayed on a plastic chair outside the restaurant and waited.

A man walked down the street, shuffling along in poor shoes and carrying a satchel that was tattered and worn. He walked slowly and his clothes hung about his bony frame, and Adaugo had tucked her feet under the chair then to make space for him and tightened her grip on her handbag. He reminded her of a homeless person, and she suddenly felt unsafe around someone who might be desperate. As she watched him move closer to her, from the opposite direction a pair of young men walked quickly towards the older man. Immersed in conversation and shouting back and forth to each other, they didn't see the older man until they were upon him. In an instant, the older man was splayed out on the sidewalk, his things scattered about. Without even the slightest hint of an apology, the two men continued walking past the man they had collided with, shouting at him over their shoulders in what was translated from pidgin English to mean, "Watch out, old man; you don't belong here, get off the streets and stay out of the way!"

Adaugo was immediately on her feet, rushing to the man's side and horrified by what she had just witnessed. How could the two men have been so callous and cruel? As she helped the man to his feet and checked that he was alright, she noticed his satchel had spilled on the ground. Gingerly, she reached out to help him collect the contents of the bag from the sidewalk and was amazed to see a collection of scholarly texts and leather-bound journals. She looked at the man then, and he saw her question in her eyes. As if in response to the question he saw there, he said, "Yes, they are mine, they are my books. And yes, I read them."

Adaugo was ashamed then. In the same way she had witnessed the two young men treating the older man like rubbish, she too had judged him as a desperate homeless man, and dismissed his value immediately.

"What do you do, sir?" she asked him then. "What is your business?"

"I own an accounting firm, and I keep the books for some of the city's larger corporations. It is fascinating work, and I have been doing it all my life."

"I'm sorry," Adaugo said. "You are clearly a professional and a scholar, and I am sorry that I looked at you as if you were something less."

"It's a common mistake people make," the old man said. "I dress like a street person, but have the mind of a scholar and the heart of a warrior."

"It is interesting to me that your outward appearance does not match your profession. Why is that, sir?"

Adaugo asked.

The older man simply smiled and then said, "I find it is an excellent way to learn the character of others. I see the judgment in the eyes of people who pass me, and then every once in a while I find someone like you, who wants to see deeper than what is on the surface. There are some weeks that go by when no one looks at me as anything but a homeless street person. But I never let it bother me."

"And why is that?" Adaugo pressed.

"I learned long ago that you may be the only person who believes in you, and that just has to be enough sometimes. I know who I am and what I am capable of, and that is enough for me," the older man concluded, and began to shuffle away.

As Adaugo resumed her seat then and waited for Anozie to arrive, she was struck by the significance of what she just witnessed. Every person, regardless of what they look like on the outside or the appearance they give, has something to teach us. The two men rushing away from the man they had knocked over had not been humble enough to learn any lesson from this wise man they viewed as inferior. *But if we stay humble, we will be able to learn something of value, even something small, from every person.*

Adaugo thought about that lesson as she looked out the window and found herself letting go of her frustration towards Abdul. Even Abdul, with his annoying office behavior, was a person who had something to teach her, and she knew that giving him respect was the right thing to do. Looking away from the window, she saw that Abdul was done with his calls and Bola quickly swooped in to grab the phone, pushing down Abdul's mobile phone in the process.

"Sorry *o*," she said in a tone that signified that she was really not sorry and if given the chance, she would probably adorn his cheeks with a slap for wasting her time.

As she quickly pulled out a squeezed A4 sheet from her brown bag, Adaugo sat back and pondered where her life was going. Between her university days and now, she felt she had become a different person from who she was meant to be. She did not hear much from Herself anymore and she felt her life drifting in a direction over which she had no control.

Now at twenty-three years of age, she had what seemed like a good job to everyone else. Hers was a job which some of her peers wished they had and she also had Anozie, an attractive, well-built, six-foot-two-inch, light-skinned telecoms engineer in his late twenties who seemed to have his life all planned out. Everyone kept telling her how lucky she was to land such a dashing guy and also have a job, especially with the high rate of youth unemployment; but deep down inside she did not feel so lucky.

If anything, she felt trapped in a life that was not hers, a life where she was not calling the shots. She felt that she was not living; rather, she was merely existing and trying hard to fit into society's definition of success.

Her mother, Ngozi, did not help matters by always reminding her of the need to get married, often citing the fact that she had already given birth to Adaugo and Ifeoma by the time she was Adaugo's age. Ngozi never hid her happiness and approval of Anozie, whose parents were well-to-do and, most importantly, Igbos. Although she had never openly voiced her disapproval of John, her Edo ex-boyfriend, and Wale, who she was still very close to, you could tell she had not been impressed with either of them from the look on her face when Adaugo's male friends came to visit her.

One year Tunde, another former classmate of hers, had come to their house on Valentine's Day with a cake to pledge his love for her, and the look Ngozi gave the young man was enough to tell him that she was only tolerating his presence for the sake of keeping the peace. Left to her, she may have emptied a bucket of water on the young man's head, cake and all.

When Adaugo finally introduced Anozie to her parents on a sunny Saturday, four months ago, her mother did all but sing and made sure he was very comfortable. She even offered to leave them in the sitting room alone to talk. This was something she had never done with her previous boyfriends and male visitors. In the past, Ngozi had always stayed in the sitting room pretending to check her mobile phone, even though Adaugo knew full well that she was only there to make sure there was no funny business going on, as she called it, and to ensure that the men knew where their boundaries sat.

Anozie was a great guy, very loving, generous and kind. He often shared his dreams of conquering the telecoms sector with Adaugo and would end with the words, "We are going to be rich, baby, and I will build a house bigger than a palace and adorn you with all the beautiful things you wish for, my princess."

And yet, being treated like a princess was not what Adaugo wanted. She did not want to be adorned and certainly did not want to spend the rest of her life living in a palatial house. She wanted to be more, she *had* to be more, and more importantly, and she knew she *could* be more. She needed to do this to be her authentic self for the sake of her sanity, peace of mind and weight, which in recent days seemed only to go in the upward direction. Food now seemed to be the only thing that almost filled the void which the absence of Herself had left.

She had to do something about this growing dissatisfaction, and quickly too. She resolved in her mind that she would make sure something would change soon as she picked up the office phone to make her sales calls for the day.

CHAPTER TWENTY-TWO

IT WAS INDEPENDENCE Day, a public holiday, and Adaugo sat on the veranda of her house. She had been restless and had trouble sleeping the night before, tossing and turning for most of the night, so after morning prayers she had decided to relax and enjoy the cool breeze of early morning. She wrapped her hands around herself as she tightened the belt of her purple dressing gown and observed the quiet street below her, three floors down. Beginning to warm up, she took a seat on one of the pink plastic chairs to clear her thoughts and perhaps relieve the slight headache she was beginning to feel.

As she rubbed her temple, she noticed that the shop owners were beginning to open for the day's business. Female street hawkers carrying mostly bread, *akara* (bean cake), and cooked beans in metal pots, walked along and announced their presence to prospective buyers, mostly young bachelors who could not be bothered with making breakfast themselves. She observed the activities below which were starting to pick up as the minutes rolled by.

It was while quietly observing the activity in the street below that she noticed three pots of aloe vera plants her mother had begun to grow and saw that they were looking very dry. She went into the house, filled up a plastic jug and went back out to water the plants. As she began watering the third pot, she felt some water leaking from the pot. The aloe vera plant had broken its pot!

Normally this would be a source of frustration, especially as they had no garden to transplant the plant to and she would have to think of a bigger pot into which to move the plant, but this time she wasn't frustrated at all. She drew closer to the plant and ran her hands along its wide, green leaves being careful not to prick her fingers and marveled at the fact that the young plant had broken through its immediate environment – its plastic pot. Its roots had grown so large that the pot could no longer hold it.

As she pondered this, she began to feel a sense of awe. She felt inspired by this example in nature of a young, vibrant plant breaking through its immediate environment, its limitations, and thriving regardless of its cramped quarters. Surely this held parallels for human beings as well.

Over the years, she realized, she had allowed her environment to limit her. She had become passive and comfortable accepting what was, rather than pursuing what should be. Her mind wandered as she considered how old laws and traditions that were set by forefathers who were long buried and gone, seemed to still stretch their hands from the grave to govern most people in Nigeria.

As she made this realisation, she heard Herself for the first time after a long hiatus, and she welcomed her as Herself took her further into considering how she had been so quick to settle for less than she could be. Herself explained to her that she had not really left her all these years, but felt unempowered because She felt She was not being heard. Herself felt She could no longer get through to Adaugo. Upon hearing this explanation, Adaugo felt some shame as she remembered the energy, the excitement, the pure zest she had felt when she had read the purple book years before.

Perhaps this was why I had trouble sleeping last night, she though as she put away the plastic jug and settled back into the chair.

Adaugo was amazed that such a little plant had brought to her a lesson on why she should not allow that which was her reality to determine her future. She was in a job she did not like and living a life that dissatisfied her, but she did not need to allow this reality to become her future.

In response to this consideration, she heard Herself ask, "Do we make up our minds to pursue our dreams no matter what the cost, or do we give them up at the slightest threat of resistance? Are we willing to look foolish in order to achieve our goals, or is the impression we are creating our major concern?"

Adaugo provided no answer to Herself's questions, perhaps because she already knew what the answers were.

She also thought of the Bible stories her parents told her when she was little and remembered the story of Noah. Even though she was older now and had her subtle doubts about the validity of the story, she was still impressed by one of the morals of this story which is, God has little use for people whose main concern is what the neighbours will think. She also considered that the greatest people that live and ever lived on this earth were people who didn't care what people thought about their ideas; rather, they seemed to be people who kept on striving forward to produce results, to reach goals that they had seen in their hearts regardless of what their present circumstances were. They never gave up; they never conformed to prescribed rules or limiting, unwritten laws that were there to create a sense of security for the people who made them, and are adopted by people too timid to do otherwise.

She thought about how foolish Noah must have felt when he was building an ark in a desert; how people must have come, seen what he was building, laughed and walked away. However, according to the story, Noah did not let this stop him. Perhaps it was because he was sure of what he had on the inside.

She now thought of the articles she had read on the internet about how Walt Disney's concepts were seen as foolish at first and the fact that he actually went bankrupt in his first business endeavor, but he still went on to build a multi-million dollar company. His products were and are still appreciated by children today.

She remembered watching Mickey Mouse and Lion King when she was younger and wondered how all that could have come from one man's dreams.

Continuing to ride the current of inspiration and thoughts that tumbled around her, she thought next of Thomas Edison, who was said to have had thousands of failures before he finally succeeded in making the first light bulb, a concept still in use to this day. There were many examples of great men, but where were the female heroines in these and similar stories? Perhaps they were busy being wives to these men. Perhaps they even played a big part in their stories, but the world never seemed to read about them.

She knew she did not want to be just another man's wife, as brilliant and wonderful as it was. This was not enough for her. She wanted more.

She determined that from then on, she would stop being concerned about what her neighbours, friends and even family thought. She would begin again on the journey to find out what her purpose in life was and she would live it.

She knew she had to proceed with this wisdom because she was well aware of how easy it was for family and friends to discourage her. They had good intentions, no doubt; but it was these good intentions that were partly to blame for her current state of intense dissatisfaction. She would keep this in her heart and look for signs and lessons just like this one until she could change the status quo for good.

As she came to this decision, she felt a wave of peace fill her. She rose from the plastic seat, quickly gave the little plant a peck and muttered the words, "Thank you," before looking around to make sure no one saw her do this.

The last thing she wanted was to be mistaken for an insane person.

CHAPTER TWENTY-THREE

WALE WAS LYING in bed when he heard his phone ring. He stretched his hand across to the right hand side of his plush king size bed, slightly knocking his new girlfriend of three weeks who was still deep in her alcohol-induced sleep. He was now a Sales Executive at Netri Oil and Gas PLC, one of the nation's largest Petroleum marketing companies. At twenty-seven and after only two years in the company, he had made a reputation for himself as a talented professional to watch out for.

He was not sure why people made so much of a fuss about him but suspected that it had something to do with his amiable personality which, now, coupled with money, made him irresistible to many females. That is to say, he was irresistible to many females *except* for the one person he really wanted, Adaugo.

"Hello, it's me," Adaugo said from the other side of the line. "Are you busy?"

Wale glanced at his sleeping girlfriend, who was oblivious to what was happening around her, and decided he wasn't busy at all.

"No, I am not, I can't be too busy for you. What's

up?"

"Wale, I am a mess, I am thinking of breaking up with Anozie."

Wale did a quick mental scan to remember who Anozie was. The tall, light skinned one, he quickly remembered.

"He sounded like a great guy. Did you not introduce him to your parents some months ago? Do your parents no longer like him?"

"That's the problem… everyone apart from me feels he is the one. They all love him, but I am not so sure. I don't feel he is the one. I am just not content," Adaugo said in a panicked and exasperated tone.

"Calm down silly, have you really thought about it?"

"Well… kind of. My intuition just tells me that there should be more. Maybe I am going crazy. What do you think?"

"I think that you should trust your intuition. Remember when it saved me from trouble those days when Dr. Ayo, the mechanics lecturer, had it in for me? You told me you didn't trust that his intentions were genuine and it turned out that you were right. So, my dear, do what is in your heart. As long as you are happy, then I am happy. Just don't be too hasty. Think about it properly before you do anything rash. You don't want to break yet another heart, Adaugo…"

"And whose heart have I broken in the past?" Adaugo asked.

"Well… let's just leave that topic for now, my dear," Wale said.

"Okay, I will do as you have advised. No rashness or sudden decisions. Let me get off the phone and leave you now to attend to the woman by your side."

"How are you so sure I have a woman by my side?" Wale asked, feigning anger.

"I know you… *ashewo*, prostitute. I know you. Moreover, I can hear her breathing from here," she said jokingly.

"Okay *o*, if you say so," Wale replied, wondering if she could really hear the sound of his girlfriend's breathing. If she could, she must have some form of dog-like hearing because the girl sleeping next to him wasn't snoring.

"I will let you know how it goes, okay?"

"Okay, please do. You take care of yourself," Wale said, lingering a bit before hanging up.

He kept his mobile phone on the bedside table on his side and glanced at his new girlfriend, who was now stirring and was relieved she had not woken up during his phone conversation as he was not ready to provide any long explanations as to whom he had been speaking to.

A little ray of hope flickered with the possibility that he and Adaugo, who he still carried a torch for all these years, could actually still be together. He quickly dismissed that thought when he remembered how he felt when he finally asked her out right before their fourth year industrial training, and her response was that she felt they were better as friends because she had started seeing some guy whose name he could not remember.

He had done all he could to disguise the hurt he felt at the time. The relationship with "what's his name" had not worked out, but he knew he was not going to let himself feel that kind hurt again. Still, even with all his resolutions, he could never completely deny his feelings for her. He knew deep down she felt the same way for him. So what was holding her back? He couldn't quite figure it out. *Only time will tell*, he thought as he lay back in bed.

As Wale settled back into bed, the eyes of Kemi, his girlfriend, snapped open as she quietly considered the conversation she had just been privy to, using sleep as a disguise and thought, "Who the hell is 'my dear' and why is she calling my boyfriend at 7:00am?" All of these thoughts had run through her mind as she had continued to pretend that she was asleep.

CHAPTER TWENTY-FOUR

A DAUGO SAT ON her seat in her office and continued browsing on her desktop computer. She liked arriving at work early, even only thirty minutes early, before the start of work, so she could gather her thoughts and plan her day. She decided to look at her bank account to see how her savings and investment portfolio was looking and decided that she liked what she saw.

She had continued with the savings culture from that day, five years ago, when she had decided she would start saving towards her future. She was glad that even with the Nigerian stock market bubble of 2009, her portfolio had not really been hit. For some reason she just intuitively knew when to enter and sell a stock. Maybe it was as a result of the market being unreasonably bullish, so everything she touched soared in price. The few loses she made were because she went against Herself's suggestions and held on to a stock, and only she was blame for that.

Now the market was gradually picking up, but there was mass apathy for investing in shares and she couldn't blame anyone for that. She knew a number of her friends who got in late and lost millions of naira. Some stories were told of people who committed suicide after they learned that their hard-earned money had gone down the drain. Others who collected peoples' money to trade on their behalf, with the promise of astronomical profits, were still at large from police men.

She was happy she was still in the green, mostly because she now stayed out of the capital market and did more of fixed deposits.

In the process of doing her mental calculations, she did not notice Abdul standing behind her, staring into her computer screen. It was only when he cleared his throat that she was startled and quickly toggled to a different window.

"Hmmm, this small girl, you have money *o*... Where did you get all this money from? I know it is not your salary because you have only been here for six months and even if you saved all your salary, you would not have half of this. Tell me, which Alhaji have you been screwing? You know I don't judge. I myself am not innocent you know..." Abdul said winking.

"Well, Abdul, first of all, it is rude of you to look over into someone's screen, especially if you were not invited. Secondly, I am not screwing any Alhaji, you dirty man. I have been saving for something in the future and I have been doing this for five years now, so please get your mind out of the gutter."

"Five years? With no job? How is that possible? I have been working for three years now and I have no savings. My wife nags me about this, but I don't know where she wants me to get the money from when she knows I need to buy new suits for work and entertain my friends every Friday. Why else am I a banker if I cannot meet up to expectations?" Abdul said. Then he became distracted by a text message he had just received.

"But whose expectations though? Who are these people you always feel the need to impress?" Adaugo asked.

"I have to prove that I have made it in life," Abdul answered, beginning to sound more defensive.

"But what do you have to prove to them? You don't have a car, Abdul; your wife picks you up from work and sometimes you strategically go and visit customers whose offices are located close to your house so that Ugorgi, the branch car driver, can drop you off at home and on the other days, you take a bus in your designer suit. Do your friends have cars?"

"Yes, they do," Abdul replied, shifting uneasily.

"Do they own their own houses or are they still paying rent?" Adaugo asked.

"Two are paying rent and the other two have built their own houses," Abdul replied.

"I bet you pay for most of the drinks when you hang out, right?"

"Well... most of the time. They offer to pay, but I decline," Abdul replied.

"So who is fooling whom now? You have been spending your hard earned money on people who are doing better than you and have achieved more, all in the name of putting up a front. Are you sure they don't laugh at you behind your back? They must think you are very foolish for doing this when they drive home in their luxury cars and you hop on the bus back home to your wife and kids.

"I read a book a while ago, *The Richest Man in Babylon*, and one particular paragraph has stayed with me all these years. It goes like this: 'Wealth, like a tree, grows from a tiny seed. The first copper you save is the tree from which your tree will grow. The sooner you plant the seed, the sooner the tree will grow. The care with which you water that tree with consistent savings, the sooner you may rest in contentment under its shade.'"

Abdul looked blankly at Adaugo, as if he didn't understand the significance of this parable in his own circumstances. So Adaugo continued to spell it out for him.

"Abdul, you need to start saving," she said. "Start with 10% of your monthly salary. At first you may feel like you are unable to survive on this, but once you do this for the first two months, you will find out that you are able to live comfortably. Cut out this suit-buying habit of yours, I don't even notice the difference when I look at you. To me and most people, a black suit is a black suit. Not many people care if you wear three different black suits made by the biggest designers. People are usually too busy to care, to be perfectly honest with you, Abdul. Just imagine how much you can save every month if you do this and please stop paying for all the drinks every time, you are not Father Christmas. Abdul... are you there? Are you with me?" Adaugo turned to her left to look at Abdul who now had a very grave look on his face.

"Are you okay Abdul?" she asked.

"Yes, I am, I need to step out for a bit... I will be back," he replied.

"Where are you off to? It is almost resumption and we have a staff meeting in ten minutes," Adaugo said, pointing to her wristwatch.

"I will be back. I need to speak to my wife," Abdul said as he rushed out of his seat. He almost knocked down the black office telephone in his haste.

CHAPTER TWENTY-FIVE

A T 8:00AM, THE entire Triumph Bank branch team of six, made up of Adaugo; Mr. Adebayo, the branch manager; Lorraine; Christina, the Personal Banking Consultants; Bola and Abdul, met for their weekly status meeting upstairs in Mr. Adebayo's office.

The meeting usually followed the same format. Mr. Adebayo would start by cascading any information or new intelligence obtained at the regional sales meeting and then he would ask each member of the team to provide updates on how many accounts they had opened since their last meeting, after which they would talk about their pipes and evaluate what percentage of their monthly sales target they had met.

These Monday meetings were usually a source of stress and tension to all members of the team as, over time, the meetings had mutated from a team meeting into an avenue for naming and shaming underperformers. It was also the worst part of Adaugo's work week because it meant that, once again, she had to explain to the entire branch why she was not meeting her target. She was in the process of thinking about what excuse to use this week when Mr. Adebayo called her name.

"Adaugo, are you here with us?"

"Yes, Mr. Adebayo," Adaugo replied.

"Where are you with your sales target?" Mr. Adebayo asked with a sneer on his face.

"45%... I have brought in 90,000 dollars out of my 200,000 dollar target so far, sir," she replied with her head bowed. She could not bear to look at her branch manager's face.

"Wait...only 90,000 dollars so far? Why are you a pretty girl? What do you have all these alluring curves for?" Mr. Adebayo barked. "Can you not see your mates meeting their targets? Do you need me to spell out how you need to conduct yourself in front of these men so you can get their money? You need to use what you have to get what you want, and you have an abundance of it. Stop wasting it on your chewing gum boyfriend!"

"So, you want me to sleep with the men?" Adaugo asked.

"Whatever you do, just bring in the money and make me proud."

He continued asking other members of the team about their progress and tongue-lashing the underperformers in their midst, but by that point Adaugo was no longer listening.

After the meeting she sat at her desk and considered all she had heard. She had heard stories of the lengths sales staff, male and female included, went to in order to hit their targets but she had never seen nor heard of a branch manager actually suggesting this.

She decided that she had to start planning her exit from this place, the earlier the better, as she struggled to hold in the hot tears which were beginning to well up in her eyes.

CHAPTER TWENTY-SIX

HAKEEM SAT IN the banking hall waiting to be attended to. He wondered why he had not been able to see any of the bank's sales staff after twenty minutes of waiting. Even though one of the cashiers had informed him that the sales team was in a meeting upstairs with the branch manager, the cashier had also said the meeting would only last ten minutes. Now, twenty minutes later, no one seemed to be coming downstairs. He began regretting making the journey to this branch and thought that perhaps he should have gone to the Apapa branch instead. It was certainly bigger than this branch.

In truth, he had booked an appointment at the Apapa branch but for some reason he could not quite figure out, something put him off that branch and kept urging him to come to this branch instead. At first he fought it because it did not make logical sense, considering that he lived close to Apapa, at least closer to Apapa than Isolo. However when his elder brother, a petroleum products marketer, announced that morning that he was going to Isolo to see one of his customers and offered to give Hakeem a lift, he didn't fight it. He just picked up his documents which were in a light blue plastic bag and got into the passenger seat of the black SUV.

Now sitting in the banking hall, sipping water from the plastic cup the cashier handed him, he wasn't so sure. He would give it another five minutes and leave this place, he decided, crumbling the now empty cup in his hands and tossing it in the bin.

He was about to leave when he heard an unfamiliar, female voice call out his name in a formal tone.

"Good morning, Mr. Kofa."

He stopped in his tracks and turned around in the direction of the voice. His eyes met a young woman in her early twenties, dressed in a blue skirt suit with a white camisole. He was a sucker for women in suits. He regarded her briefly as he pondered how she got to know his name and remembered that he gave the details to the cashier when he came in. The cashier must have passed his details to the tall, pretty lady standing in front of him.

"Yes, but please called me Hakeem," he replied as he extended his hand to reach hers for a handshake.

Adaugo was taken aback by his offer of a handshake, particularly as she guessed that, from his name, he was a Muslim and from what she understood about most of the devout ones, they certainly did not shake women's hands. Additionally, the man standing in front of her looked especially devout, she was genuinely curious as to his behavior.

He wore a cream, well-starched kaftan, which suited him quite well. His skin was a fine cross between the colour of chocolate and vanilla and she decided that, after a quick mental map of his height compared to that of Anozie, he was six-feet-four-inches at least.

"Hi, I am Adaugo. I am very pleased to meet you and I give you my sincere apologies for the delay. Our meeting ran a little longer than it should have."

"It is okay, now you are here. I was beginning to wonder if I should have gone to the Apapa branch, but now I am glad I didn't," he said with a coy smile.

"I too am glad you didn't," Adaugo replied with a forced smile.

Hakeem took another look at the young woman and noticed that she looked very sad and although she had tried to hide it, he could see her eyes were filled with tears. He wasn't a stranger to this look. He had seen it so many times on his mother's face every time she tried to hide the fact that his father had beaten her the night before.

He also recognised that look the day she drove back that fateful morning after she had learned from her doctor that she had ovarian cancer. She had lost her four-year battle with the disease a year before and it was only now that he was finally starting to feel he was starting to move forward with his life.

"Chuma told me you were interested in opening one of my preferred accounts. Do you know which one you want or do you want me to go through them with you upstairs?" Adaugo asked, interrupting his thoughts.

"Yes, I know what product I need, I have all my relevant documents," Hakeem replied.

"Alright then, let us go upstairs and get those forms filled out so you can be on your way," Adaugo replied as she led the way upstairs with Hakeem contentedly following behind, admiring the view she provided him.

Upstairs they filled the relevant forms and in the

process she gathered that he wanted the account so he could put away some foreign currency and pay his school fees for a Master's Degree programme he planned to enroll in later that year, in September.

Even though it was only January, Hakeem wanted to start early with building his account balance so that when he finally received his admission letter, the tuition fee payment process would be smooth and hitch free.

Adaugo admired his vision and volunteered that she herself had never considered furthering her education, especially as her first degree had been such a nightmare to finish.

Hakeem agreed that it was the same for him and that was one of the reasons he was keen to try out a different style of learning. He also opined that there were usually more opportunities abroad and he had friends who, after their degrees were completed, had gone on to get good jobs abroad.

The idea of leaving Nigeria and leaving her dead beat job excited her and she obtained more information from Hakeem as she completed his application forms.

When they were done, she promised she would send his application to the compliance team and then she would send him a text to let him know when his account was opened. She also advised him that the process would take 24-48 hours.

"That is fine with me. Please make sure you text me to let me know," Hakeem replied as he stood from his seat.

"It was lovely meeting you, Hakeem; let me walk you out," Adaugo replied, extending her hand.

"The pleasure is all mine, Adaugo," Hakeem replied and they made their way downstairs to the banking hall.

Hakeem waved to Chuma, the cashier, and made his way out the sliding glass doors.

Adaugo winked her thanks to Chuma and made her way back upstairs. As she walked she considered the possibility of studying abroad and quickly dismissed it. It was going to be too difficult she decided, and redirected her thoughts then to gathering Hakeem's application forms to scan to the compliance department.

Chapter Twenty-Seven

THE FOLLOWING FRIDAY evening, Kemi and Wale met for dinner at Cherries Restaurant, a local favourite, after which they intended to retire to Wale's house for the weekend.

"I'll have a chicken salad and a glass of your freshly pressed orange juice," Kemi said, ordering from the waiter.

"And for me, a bottle of Guinness Extra Stout, and the boiled rice with goat meat pepper soup, please," said Wale.

To Wale, Kemi seemed to have the energy of a person perpetually consuming energy drinks, though he knew she didn't. *Where did all of her energy come from then?* She seemed to eat so little, and he worried that she was not nourishing herself properly. He worried about her health, but at the same time he admired her taste in food and her ability to order things he didn't think he could stomach, not to mention things he didn't think he'd even enjoy. He often wondered where she developed her fine taste because from what he knew about her, she did not come from a privileged background. Also, she had never set her foot outside the shores of Nigeria, except for that one time she travelled for two weeks to South Africa to shoot a music video for one of the most popular Nigerian hip hop artists. She came back after the two week trip with an accent which was a cross between Jamaican and British, which was confusing to Wale because he did not understand how it was possible for someone to acquire a new accent within two weeks.

Nevertheless, he humoured her and didn't joke with her about her new accent. Instead he patiently waited and was silently relieved when the accent faded away after a few hours of being back home.

It took less than ten minutes for the cheerful waiter to bring their meals and as he began eating the spicy dish he had ordered, Wale had to accommodate the heat of the dish by blowing air through his mouth at intervals, desperately trying to counterbalance the burning sensation on his tongue. And that was when he noticed that Kemi wasn't eating. He found this strange even for her and watched her mindlessly picking at her salad and dropping it with her fork, sighing periodically and looking altogether bored.

"What is the matter, Kemi? Why are you not eating? Is something bothering you? Did the auditions go wrong? I know you told me you had one today," he finally asked.

"No, my auditions went well actually. My agent says he has high hopes for this one," Kemi replied, still picking at her food.

"Then what is it? You are not eating and I am getting worried." Wale prayed silently that she would not blurt out something game-changing, like news of an unexpected pregnancy, because he didn't think he could handle something such as that. He had already had that experience many years ago, with Lara, and ultimately it had led to their breakup.

Lara's pregnancy had turned out to be false, a test that she devised for him to determine his level of commitment to her after two years of dating. Her test worked. The words exchanged between them while she was pretending to be carrying his baby gave her all the signs she needed to know that he had no plans for a serious relationship. They parted ways shortly after.

He wasn't looking forward to facing something similar with Kemi, especially since he was only recently beginning to develop feelings for her, though her body language over dinner was vaguely reminiscent of Lara's right before she had shared her pregnancy news.

"Tell me, tell me what is wrong. I know something is bothering you," Wale implored.

"Are you cheating on me, Wale?" Kemi blurted out, noisily dropping her cutlery on the porcelain white ceramic plate.

The noise attracted the attention of other diners, who were now beginning to look in their direction.

"I don't understand what you mean, Kemi. Cheating on you *ke*, how?" Wale replied, looking confused and mentally scanning his brain for anything that may have provoked such a thought.

"Do not play on my intelligence, Wale. I know your type," Kemi continued.

"First of all, I find that comment very annoying. What do you mean by 'type'?" Wale asked.

"Do not change the subject. Who is this 'dear' you were speaking to the last time I slept over at your house? I didn't want to mention it until we saw each other face to

145

face again. *Oya* tell me! You think I didn't hear you *abi*, is that so? Tell me now!" Kemi was becoming visibly angry.

"I don't get you. What 'dear' are you referring to…?" Wale meant to continue but paused when he realised that Kemi was referring to. She must have overheard the conversation he had with Adaugo. He did a quick mental calculation on the best way to respond without further infuriating his five-foot-eleven-inch model girlfriend.

"The phone call was with Adaugo, my former classmate. I thought I had told you about her before," Wale lied. He knew full well that he intentionally had never told Kemi about his closeness with Adaugo as their friendship had been the reason for the demise of some of his past relationships. His ex-girlfriends, after hearing the way he spoke about her, always seemed to come to one conclusion – he was still in love with her. The process for his girlfriends to reach the same conclusion took a varying length of time, but ultimately they all left him because of it. None of them wanted to be in a relationship that was bound to be complicated by Wale's feelings for another woman, and he couldn't say he blamed them.

He decided he was not going to let that happen with Kemi, so he had never told her about Adaugo when they started dating. But as he sat there over dinner watching his girlfriend gesticulating even more angrily with each passing second, it occurred to him that perhaps he had been wrong to hide this from her. Even worse, it might be too late now to come clean and restore his relationship with Kemi; her doubts were looming large.

146

Chapter Twenty-Eight

ADAUGO RODE PATIENTLY in the back seat of the black, 2008 Toyota Corolla saloon car. In the driver's seat sat Ugorji, the branch driver, who was quietly maneuvering the car through the busy lunch hour traffic of Ikeja, the capital city of Lagos State. They were on their way to see a new prospect, Mr. Julius Omisore, who rang the office earlier that morning requesting to open a Preferred Current Account. He had received one of the bank fliers through his door and for the first time in a long while, Adaugo was beginning to feel like her efforts to leave fliers at her neighbours' houses were beginning to pay off.

Her colleagues had laughed at her when she told them she planned to put the fliers out but now, sitting in the car, she was happy she had done it. She thought about Mr. Omisore as they drove and wondered how much he would pay; more than that, she was curious about what he did for a living.

Ugorji briefly interrupted her thoughts by asking if she wanted to buy gala sausage rolls, a snack which was usually peddled by hawkers wherever a traffic jam assembled on the streets of Lagos. Adaugo often wondered where the hawkers came from because they seemed so efficient at knowing when a traffic jam was about to build up and showed up promptly, shoving their wares through the glass until a driver succumbed to their beckoning, either due to hunger or due to boredom from having to sit in the car waiting for traffic almost indefinitely.

She also wondered about Ugorgi's helpful suggestion that she should purchase some snacks. Perhaps he suggested it because he knew that there was no way she would buy some without buying for him. He was quite the cunning man, but Adaugo did not hold this against him. If she were on a salary of 35,000 naira with a family of four to support, she too would look for creative ways to obtain some free lunch.

"Yes, please tell the guy to bring two packets of gala and please check the expiry date," Adaugo replied.

"What about Lacasera drink or Fanta? Would you not need something with which to wash the food down?" Ugorgi asked, smiling through the front mirror.

"Yes Ugorgi, ask him to bring one bottle of Lacasera and one drink for you, too."

"Thank you, madam. God bless you," Ugorgi replied excitedly.

"No problem. God bless you, too," Adaugo replied as she reached out for her drink and packet of gala, leaving one on the dashboard for Ugorgi to eat.

When they arrived at the office complex, she dialed the potential customer's number using her mobile phone. Mr. Omisore had left his number with her when he called the office some hours before to request the account.

"Hello, this is Julius Omisore," the man spoke with a subtle Yoruba accent.

"Good afternoon sir, this is Adaugo from Triumph bank, we spoke some hours ago. I am at your office complex."

"Oh, the banker, yes, yes! I will send my secretary Mary to let you in. I am sorry our offices are a bit confusing. Just wait beside the mobile phone shop. Mary will be down shortly," Mr. Omisore instructed.

"How will I recognise Mary, your secretary? There are a number of people here," Adaugo asked, sounding perplexed.

"You will know Mary, do not worry. She never smiles," Mr. Omisore chuckled.

True to Mr. Omisore's promise, Adaugo recognised Mary immediately, because of the serious look on her face. The woman, who could not have been taller than five-foot-four-inches, had one of the most pensive looks she had ever seen. At her height and by the few silver grey lines at the top of her neatly packed but otherwise jet black hair, Adaugo could easily place her at an age range of between forty-two and forty-eight at the most.

As Mary led her into the office, Adaugo did a quick mental run-through of the bank's product benefits to ensure she could deliver a befitting sales pitch if Mr. Omisore needed one. She suspected he wouldn't, especially as he called her to request the visit, not the other way around.

They entered the well-furnished office, a sharp contrast to its outer environment, and Mary knocked quietly and let Adaugo into Mr. Omisore's office.

"Good afternoon, Mr. Omisore, it is a pleasure to meet

you," Adaugo said to the average-sized man who was now standing and walking towards her to extend a handshake.

"Good afternoon, my banker. Please call me Julius, and thank you for coming on such a short notice. Please take a seat. Do you need a drink? Water, juice, a soft drink?"

"No problem Julius, and no, don't worry about the drink. I just had one in the car."

They went on to discuss the account details and Mr. Omisore issued a check for the opening balance after completing his forms. As she began to pack up her belongings and completed forms to leave Mr. Omisore's office, he asked her to sit back for a friendly chat.

This should be interesting, Adaugo thought. She sat back down, feeling through her hand bag to make sure her pepper spray was still intact. The can of pepper spray had been a gift from Ivie when she heard that Adaugo had taken a bank sales job. Adaugo remembered the look of innocent bemusement on Ivie's face when she unwrapped her gift to reveal the bright, cylindrical can.

"You never know when you would need it, babe, especially as a pretty girl. Those randy rich men will be on you like flies on a pile of shit. You need to be prepared," she had said.

"Thanks, I pray I don't ever need it," Adaugo had replied.

Now she was thankful for the assurance her friend's little gift gave her as she settled in for a "friendly chat" with her newest rich client. Whether he was randy or not, in addition to being rich, remained to be seen.

"So my dear banker, what do you want to do with

your life? You sound too intelligent to be stuck in this job. I watched you deliver your sales pitch instead of coming in with a half unbuttoned shirt like some of your colleagues in your industry. Have you thought about your life plan? By the way, please relax. I have a daughter your age."

On hearing this, Adaugo let her hand relax, the one that had been stealthily grasping the pepper spray can, and silently said a prayer of thanks before she continued.

"Well, Mr. Omisore... Julius, I mean. I have been waiting for my big idea. I have done some laptop supplies, share trading before the stock market burst and have saved some money...and I still do and plan to continue to save until I get my big business idea."

"Sounds like a good plan, but we both know that this environment of ours is not the most conducive for ideas generation. Have you considered travelling abroad to further your studies? Perhaps the experience of living in a different country could provide you with ideas to bring back home."

"This study abroad idea again, twice in one week, Adaugo! You need to start considering..." Herself started to say before Adaugo quickly cut her off.

"Funny thing sir, the idea has popped into my head a number of times this week alone," she replied.

"Well, perhaps you should start considering it or do you have one boyfriend deceiving you here?" Julius asked with a wink.

"Not exactly, sir... I just need to be sure it is the right path for me."

"This may be Allah speaking to you through me, you never know; and since you say you have been considering

151

it a lot this week, then you should consider it a bit more."

"Sir, I thought you were a Christian," said Adaugo, now rechecking the forms Julius had signed.

"My wife is a Muslim, and I practice the Jewish religion," Julius said.

"So how do you make it work? Two different religions in one household?" Adaugo asked, looking confused.

"We make it work just because we want to. Religion should never be a barrier when it comes to love. She goes to her mosque and comes back; I go to the synagogue and come back. I don't love her any less because of the religion she chooses to practice, and she doesn't love me any less. If anything, it gives us more to discuss and with marriage, you need to keep things interesting.

"This is why I find it amazing that even within Christianity people insist that their spouses must be Catholics, Anglicans or even Protestants and Pentecostals. I find it a big mess that we can't all live together, in peace in our world. Look at the 9/11 bombing, look at all these wars taking place in the name of religion.

"Do you remember the story of the tower of Babel? I am sure it is in your Bible. We have it in our holy book, the Torah, in Bereishis; that is, the book of Genesis. Never mind, my banker; let me not bore you. I know you have to be on your way and I don't want you to get stuck in traffic," Julius said, with some hesitation.

"No sir, you are not boring me. I find it very interesting. Please carry on with the Tower of Babel story. I remember reading the Bible story from when I was little," Adaugo replied, encouraging him to continue.

"If you insist, I will continue. According to the Torah,

after the flood where Noah built an ark that saved a handful of people on earth, man had again begun to multiply and fill the earth. They all spoke one language and understood one another well. The generations of people before the flood had been interested only in themselves; they thought of themselves as super-men and super-women and lived each one for himself or herself alone; they used violence and force against their weaker neighbours, paying no attention to laws and rules.

"However, this new generation of mankind was different. They stressed the opposite code of living. The individual did not count for himself; he counted only as part of the community, and he had to subject his own interests to those of the group. Had they confined themselves to this kind of social life, all might have been well. But the problem is that they overdid it."

"How so, sir?" Adaugo asked.

"They had tremendous strength that grew out of their organisation, and goodwill made them proud, but the problem is that their pride made them turn against God. So they decided to build a tower which was to reach to heaven, to make them equal to God, and at the same time, to make it possible for them to stay together. Now the fact that they built this tower was not a bad thing, it was the intent behind the building of this tower that was bad. Are you with me?" Julius asked.

"Yes, I am…" Adaugo responded, listening intently.

"Now, what was the underlying reason for their strength? It was the fact that they spoke one language. Their unity was their strength and this came about through the speaking of one language. God knew that the best way to divide them was to introduce different languages, thus destroying their arrogance by destroying their ability to understand one another. He, therefore, confused the people by splitting them up into seventy different nations and tribes, each with a language of its own. This where the name Babel came from; it literally means confusion.

"When this happened, the project of the Tower had to be given up. The various groups migrated in different directions and settled in all parts of the world. The Tower itself was partly burned and partly swallowed by the earth.

"Maybe we as a race are not supposed to be united, maybe it is God's will that we must always look for differences in one another before looking at what we all share in common."

"Wow... I have never thought about it that way, sir," Adaugo confessed.

"I know, most people have not, and I like the fact that you have a very curious mind and you are willing to learn. You are a special one, at least you still have your brain intact and you are curious about life. This is a good thing, and I will give you the same advice I always give my daughter: do not be afraid to go out there into the world to experience things and expand your horizon. Husbands are everywhere, so never let the society you live in limit you with its rules and regulations. Here is my card, if you decide to go travel abroad, call me and I will give you a free return ticket valid for a year. Let us call it a good will gesture towards a hardworking and curious banker." Julius smiled as he handed her his business card.

"Are you serious, sir?" Adaugo replied, looking suspiciously at the business card he handed to her.

"Yes, my daughter. I believe I was led to speak to you today. If I have learnt anything in my sixty-three years on this earth, it is that you should not ignore that still small voice in your head that tries to guide you. I have been putting off opening this account. Some of your colleagues in other branches have come to see me, but I was not interested. However, for some reason today, I could not get any rest until I took the flier you posted through my door and gave your branch a call. Now I know why. I have done my part now and I can now rest. The rest is up to you," Mr. Omisore said, getting up to see her to the door.

"God bless you, sir. Honestly, I will think about it and will also let you know when your account has been opened. It usually takes 24-48 hours but as today is a Friday, it means that your account may not be opened till Tuesday of next week. Also, our compliance managers will give you a call if they have any additional questions. I hope this is okay with you, sir."

"No problem, they are welcome to call me; I will be here," Julius replied.

He rose from his seat and saw to it that she reached the car park safely before waving goodbye.

She settled into her seat and looked at the attractive blue and gold business card with the company name "Omisore Aviation Services Ltd," written across it in navy blue font.

"Madam, should I drop you at home or do you want to go back to the branch?" Ugorgi asked, interrupting her thoughts.

"*Mba*, no let's go to the branch, I need to scan these forms before the compliance department close for the day," she responded.

"Did he open the account, Madam?" Ugorgi asked, glancing through the mirror.

"Yes, Ugorgi, he did. *Daalu*, thank you for asking," Adaugo answered with a smile.

"Thank God! I was worried because you stayed inside for so long. I was considering coming inside to check on you and to make sure you were okay," Ugorgi confessed.

"That is very kind of you, everything went well. Let me rest now please." she said.

"No problem madam, rest, I will raise the air conditioner for you."

What are the odds? she thought as Ugorgi expertly sped through the now not-so-busy Ikeja-Maryland expressway towards her branch.

CHAPTER TWENTY-NINE

THE FOLLOWING MORNING Adaugo and Obioma, who was now twenty years of age, were in the kitchen preparing *akara*, or bean cakes. The preparation involved soaking beans in water overnight and then taking the skin off of each seed by taking a handful of beans in between one's palms till all the seeds were de-skinned. Once this was done, the peeled beans were then blended with peppers, onions and a number of other ingredients until it became a paste; the paste was then deep-fried in hot oil. The process from de-skinning the beans to having a ready meal usually took about three hours, for a family of six.

Adaugo was washing the brown beans, quietly wishing that her mother had not decided to make such a complicated meal for breakfast, wishing instead for their usual, simpler breakfast of triangle-shaped sandwiches, noodles or better still, cereal. She despised making *akara* because to her it was much ado about nothing; but like the good daughter she was trying to be, she did not complain too loudly. The only thing that gave away her disgust for the task was the occasional hiss when some water poured on the kitchen floor.

As she washed the beans, she could not help considering the happenings of the week. For some reason, no matter how hard she tried, she could not get away from the thought of studying abroad, particularly after Mr. Omisore had generously offered to pay for her flight ticket. His offer had come to her out of nowhere, out of thin air, and it was something she could not stop thinking about and puzzling over. She also could not get her mind off their discussions about unity and the tower of Babel. Now that she was aware of the idea of studying abroad, it was as if the Universe was actively doing everything to show her signs that this was the right path to take.

For example, on the way back from Ikeja to her branch after meeting with Mr. Omisore, she saw a banner on the Iyana Isolo bridge with the words, "Study Abroad for your Master's Degree Programme." She could have sworn she had passed that bridge a number of times without ever noticing the sign before.

And then, just that morning, the newspaper vendor dropped off the Saturday Conscience Newspaper and a flier dropped out of the bulky newspaper with yet another study abroad message.

She knew from the principle of recognition that, "In order for something to become one's reality, one must first recognise it." Now that she had recognised it, solutions seemed to be everywhere, almost overwhelmingly so.

Adaugo was so lost in thought she did not notice that Obioma, who was previously in the kitchen store room, was now standing right beside her and staring at her.

"Adaugo, *gini ka ina eche*, what are you thinking about?" she asked.

"I am not sure what you are talking about, *biko hapu m*; please leave me alone," Adaugo lied.

"You can say it is nothing but I have been standing here staring at you and you didn't even notice me; so whatever you may have been thinking about must have been serious. *Bia*, come, is it Anozie?" Obioma asked looking suspiciously at her sister.

"Anozie *kwa*! *Mba o*, no... it is not him, I am just considering a lot of things right now."

"A lot of things like what? Tell me now... Maybe I can help," Obioma offered.

As much as Adaugo loved the fact that Obioma was so concerned, she was getting irritated by her relentless and tireless questions.

"*Puoro m n'uzo*, clear out of my path, I need to start grinding these beans before Mummy comes and wonders what is keeping us. Don't worry, I will tell you once I have figured it out," she promised.

Obioma was not happy with this response and scrunched up the nose on her otherwise delicate and slim face. Sometimes Adaugo could not believe how quickly Obioma had grown up, changing from a relatively skinny child to a glowing, tall beauty in seemingly no time at all. The beautiful girl standing before her then was not happy and was not hiding it.

"*Nsogbu adiro*, no problem, Miss Secretive; I will still find out, whether you want to tell me right now or not! I don't even care *sef*," Obioma replied, walking away and obviously miffed that she was not immediately let in on Adaugo's suspected secret.

Adaugo did not blame her for being frustrated. If she were in Obioma's shoes, she too would be annoyed.

CHIKAMSO C. EFOBI

Adaugo continued watching the *akara* mixture as it began to swirl noisily around the inside of the large white blender.

CHAPTER THIRTY

THE FOLLOWING MONDAY, Adaugo arrived at her office an hour earlier than she usual. The bank branch security man looked at her with surprise when he saw her standing at the branch gate so early.

"I hope there is no problem, Madam," he said.

"No, no problem, everything is alright. I just need to get some work done early, that's all," Adaugo replied.

The security guard opened the gate and she walked inside, past the generator house, and into the empty bank branch compound. She climbed the two flights of stairs to her office, sat down, and switched on her computer. As she waited for it to power up, she pulled out her notebook and wrote down her task list.

She had come in early to do further research on universities and potential courses, including whatever fees needed to be paid. If she was going to do this, to study abroad, she needed to know how much it would cost. She had still not told anyone about it yet, rationalizing that she needed to gather the necessary facts first and make her own decision before announcing anything to her family and Anozie.

She expected some resistance, especially from her

family, as there was a general notion that if a woman got too educated, she would never find a husband because her knowledge would make her pompous and difficult to control.

After one and a half hours, she had obtained all the information she felt she needed and sent out two inquiry emails to two universities that piqued her interest, the University of Bangor, Wales and De Montfort University, Leicester. She had looked at some universities that were more popular, but had quickly dismissed them because of their exorbitant school fees. She finished just seconds before Abdul strolled into the office, whistling happily.

Abdul's whistling caused her to suspect that he must have had an interesting weekend, or else why would he be in such a light-hearted and jovial mood on a Monday morning? She started to ask, but changed her mind. She did not want to be weighed down by Abdul's complete recap of his weekend. She also noted that Abdul had changed a bit. He was no longer so loquacious and she noticed he spent less time on the phone. He had also stopped being so tied to his mobile phone. Perhaps her talk with him had worked after all. She would find out later but right now, she had more important things to think about, like how she would raise the remaining £6000 she needed to make up her tuition and accommodation fees, if she ever got admission into any of the universities she had just written to.

She didn't want to ask her father; he already had enough on his plate building a new house and paying school fees for her other three siblings.

At 10:00am she got a call from Dennis, the branch compliance officer, who informed her that Mr. Omisore's account had been opened. She thanked him and was especially happy that it had taken a short time than expected for the account to be opened. She searched her handbag for Julius' business card and dialed his mobile number.

On the second try, the number went through and a female voice answered, which confused her. Adaugo quickly took a look at her mobile phone to make sure she dialed the right number, which she had.

"Good morning, my name is Adaugo Obi. I am calling from Triumph Bank, can I please speak to Mr. Omisore?"

"Yes, I will get him for you. I am Zainab Omisore, his wife, he told me that he applied to open an account with your bank," the woman on the other end of the line said.

"Yes Madam, Thank you" Adaugo responded, wondering just how much Julius told his wife.

After a couple of minutes of waiting, Julius finally picked up the phone and she informed him that his account has been opened; additionally, she provided him with his account details.

"That was very fast; my banker; thank you for all your effort and remember what we discussed *o*!" Julius replied.

"I have not forgotten, sir. I am definitely thinking about it," Adaugo laughed.

"That is all I need to hear. Have a good day and let me know what you decide," he replied.

"I will do, sir. Have a good day, too!" she replied and hung up the call.

She took another look at her notepad and did a quick calculation of how long it would take to save up the short fall between her current savings and university tuition. She figured that if she saved the equivalent of £500 every month, she would have all the money she needed in twelve months, and that would be in time for September 2010 admission intake. It was going to be a long twelve months considering that £500 represented 80% of her monthly salary. She would have to be open to additional business opportunities to dampen the impact of such an aggressive savings plan. And, there would be no unnecessary clothing purchases and no unnecessary lunch or dinner outings; she would only buy necessary items. It needed to be done, so it would be done, she determined as she picked up the phone to follow up with other sales leads.

Chapter Thirty-One

THREE MONTHS LATER, she had finished putting away her third consecutive monthly savings into her account. By her calculations, she would need to continue saving for an additional nine months. Initially she had thought her savings plan would put a lot of strain on her lifestyle; in reality, it hadn't. She was still able to afford all her necessities and live comfortably. This made her wonder where all her money had been going to before she started saving so aggressively. Her ability to cope and even thrive brought a truth she had known for a long time to the forefront once again. It was a quote by Paulo Coelho, author of the highly-acclaimed best seller, *The Alchemist*, and in it, he said, "When you want something, all the universe conspires in helping you to achieve it."

She felt grateful that such a truth was coming to pass in her life and the illustrations of the principle in her life were exciting to observe. For example, she was getting nicer customers who were helping her meet her target, which meant she was getting more bonuses. She also got the opportunity to supply twenty units of Toshiba laptops to a company and the profit from this opportunity was sufficient for her to live on without needing to touch her salary.

Even more pleasing was the fact that she and Herself were embarking on an even closer relationship and, for the first time that she could remember, she was excited about life and work. If she had any doubts about her new path, they had all gone. She had still not mentioned her goal to Anozie, probably because she suspected it would not go well with him and he may want to break up with her. She dreaded the confrontation that may ensue, so she decided she would tell him sooner rather than later, perhaps that very evening, to be fair to him.

That evening instead of meeting at Cherries restaurant as they usually did, Anozie asked that they meet at the Protea hotel restaurant. He fancied a change, he had said. As they ate their dinner, she noticed that Anozie was very quiet, almost tense.

"Is everything okay?" Adaugo asked.
"Yeah sure... just work stress, that's all," Anozie replied, refusing to meet her eyes.

"Okay... if you say so. I have something to tell you but I am not sure how you will take it," Adaugo said after a few moments of eating in silence.

"I have something to tell you too...but you go first," Anozie said.

"Recently, I have been thinking of travelling abroad to study for my Master's degree. I have been feeling stuck, as you know. And actually this is something I have been thinking about for quite a while and have started saving some money towards it. I didn't want to mention it earlier because I wanted to be 100% sure it was what I wanted to do, and now I have no doubt," she said.

"A Master's degree? What would you use a Master's degree for? You don't need too much education, not that much, and abroad too? What a silly idea, you will not survive. There are a lot of wolves out there. Look at me, even as a man I don't think I need a Master's degree. You have a good job, why mess things up?" Anozie replied, getting angry.

"But I am not happy with the job I have and you know this," Adaugo replied, trying hard to keep her voice down.

"Are you not happy with me? I don't want you travelling anywhere. You need to kill all these airy, fairy tendencies you have. This is the real world and I will not allow this, not while you are my girlfriend. I have just a BSc degree and you want to go and get a Master's Degree, so you can be commanding me at home? You have to choose between this, your travelling idea, and us, because I can't allow you travel while we are together!" Anozie continued.

"Why? What is the big deal? It is just for a year and you can come and see me. Don't you want me to be happy?" Adaugo asked.

"I want you to be happy, but you are not travelling and that is final!" Anozie replied.

"So, what are you saying? You would rather have me stuck in a dead end job, in an unexciting life, just to be with you?"

"Well, I should be enough for you. I wonder who has been feeding you with this rubbish. Master's, my backside! Look here, young lady; if you decide to pursue this idea of yours, consider this relationship over. Now eat your food!" Anozie replied, calming down.

She had never seen him so angry throughout the time

167

they had been together. But beyond that, what shocked her the most was his blatant refusal to consider her happiness. What did it matter if she was going to get an MSc and he had only a BSc anyway? It would not change her to a different person, she would still be respectful of him.

They spent the rest of the meal in silence. Even though neither of them was speaking to the other, she knew deep down that there was no need for more words. She had decided on her path and she was taking it, with or without him. It was disappointing that he was not more supportive, but perhaps it was for the best. She had always had her doubts about their relationship, and his reaction and condescending words tonight were all that she needed to finally convince herself it was time to end it.

They finished their meal and Anozie led her to his car and got into the driver's seat. Looking across through the passenger seat, he asked her to get in but she just stood there.

"Get into the car. It is getting late and I don't want to be stuck in traffic taking you home," Anozie barked.

"Don't worry about me," Adaugo whispered.

"Sorry, I didn't hear that? Come in, and stop wasting time!" Anozie was now shouting.

"Do not worry about me, I am travelling abroad. I choose to do more with my life" Adaugo raised her voice when she spoke then, to make sure he heard her this time.

Anozie did a double take. Throughout their relationship, he had never seen her go against his word. She had always agreed with almost everything he said. He was not comfortable with this new Adaugo he was seeing for the first time.

"Fair enough then. Take care," Anozie said and drove off.

Adaugo stood there, not sure what had just happened. She felt a cold breeze blow and wrapped her arms around herself. To her left was a taxi park, so she walked over there in her high heels and took a taxi.

As she sat in the taxi, she was surprised she did not feel confused or unsettled. All she felt was a gentle sense of peace and she heard the words of Herself, saying, "You will be fine. Trust me. You will be fine." Adaugo had no doubt about this.

Chapter Thirty-Two

WHEN SHE ARRIVED at home, Adaugo went straight to her room, which she shared with her sister. She put down her handbag and fell into bed without even taking off her work clothes and shoes first. As she lay there, she tried to make sense of what had just happened with Anozie.

Even though she had her doubts about the relationship, she had stayed in the relationship a long while just to make sure she wasn't being too hasty, something she had been accused of a number of times in the past. She wished she had stuck to her gut instinct when she first began to have her doubts; now, several months later, she was back to the same point she would have been at if she had followed her instincts in the first place.

The only difference was that she now knew beyond any doubt that they were not meant to be together. It wasn't too much to ask for some support from the man who constantly professed that he was there to take care of her, was it? She now understood that he was there to take care of her as long she stayed the pretty, nice girlfriend. Any moves by her to be happy or do more with her life instigated an ultimatum. It was either him or her happiness; she could be with him, or she could grow and make herself better. She couldn't have both.

Obioma walked into the room then and, as she was undressing, sat on her bed watching Adaugo in silence. Adaugo took one look at her sister and realised that she knew.

"This one, you are sitting silently on my bed watching me; Anozie called you *abi*, isn't that so?" Adaugo asked.

"Well, yes, he did and he sounded very angry, threatening a break-up. He said I should talk you back to your senses," Obioma said.

"So are you here to talk your mad sister back to her senses? *Nsogbu adiro*, no problem. Start talking, I am listening."

"The only thing I can say is I hope you know what you are doing. This whole Master's thing. Is it enough to lose a relationship over? You can do it after you two get married. At least then you would know you are married," Obioma said softly.

"Wait… when exactly would I get to travel abroad? Would it be after our honeymoon, or during my first pregnancy or the second one? Or after two or three kids? Who would take care of the kids when I am away? I expected Anozie to be more supportive, instead he tried make me feel and look stupid for wanting more for myself. He even tried to say I was silly for wanting a Master's because even he only had a BSc. Does that even make sense? What difference would it make? Would I not be the same person?" Adaugo replied, flinging her bra into the wardrobe.

"Well… if he did that, then he is wrong. He should

want you to be happy and fulfilled. Your happiness should not be tied to him," Obioma said while she put away her sister's shoes into the wardrobe. "At least I now know what the secret is you have been keeping away from me. I support you and hope Daddy allows you to do this."

"I hope so too. Please keep this between us until I am able to confirm my admission and gather some more money. I don't want Daddy to state lack of funds as a reason against allowing me to go. It is bad enough that I have let go of their golden, future son-in-law," Adaugo replied.

"I support you, but I would act like I was not aware of your plans if anyone should ask. I don't want anyone roping me in as a bad egg. So I am with you, but in the spirit," Obioma replied.

"Fair weather sister, thanks for having my back," Adaugo joked.

"Any time," Obioma replied. She stepped out of the room then to continue the Nigerian movie she was watching on the African Magic Movie Channel.

Chapter Thirty-Three

THOUGH SHE WASN'T sharing her plans yet with her parents, Adaugo felt that she needed the support of her friends and, when the time was right, she shared her news with Ivie and Tola. Another reason she told them of her plans, perhaps the bigger reason, was that they kept asking about how her relationship with Anozie was going and she couldn't keep their breakup a secret any longer. Their responses were a mix of anger and support. Tola confessed that she had been considering the idea of leaving the country, but she was more concerned about getting a husband. Everything could wait till after that, she reasoned.

She also informed Wale over the phone. He expressed happiness that she was trying to get more done with her life. Even though Wale was saying what she wanted to hear, she felt like he was holding something back.

"Are you okay, Wale? You don't seem happy," Adaugo said.

"I am happy for you, but I don't know where this leaves us. A part of me is happy for you to pursue your dream, but I guess the knowledge that I can't just drive to your house or call you for a drink to chat once you move away makes me sad," Wale answered.

"But I am not dying, I will be one call away. By the way, you have Kemi our Miss Model, you don't need me," she replied.

"It is not the same and you know it. We have been through a lot together and you know I love you; and I know you care for me too, no matter how you try to convince yourself otherwise."

"I never said I didn't care about you, but I need you to be feel like I am doing more with my life, I need to experience somewhere different and going abroad would be the perfect opportunity. It will be like I never left. I will call, you can call me anytime you wish or whenever Kemi decides to fight with you! The fact I will be in another country changes nothing," she replied, logically.

"Have you got admission now?" Wale asked.

"Almost, they have asked for my transcript from Uni and I have applied for it."

"What about funds? Have you got all the funds you need?"

"I am almost there. The only thing I'm still not sure about yet is how to break the news to my parents. I have managed to keep it a secret these past few months, but I need to tell them soon."

"You're right. You need to tell them, and soon. I am sure you will be fine. Let me know if you need anything."

"No worries, will do. Thanks for being there," Adaugo replied and hung up the phone.

CHAPTER THIRTY-FOUR

ZAINAB OMISORE ROLLED over in the fluffy, king-sized bed she shared with Julius, her husband. It was a Saturday morning and she could hear the distant chirping of a bird sitting on a tree outside her window. She particularly liked the chirping of birds because it reminded her of her days as a teenager living in Kaduna.

She looked across at her husband who was snoring peacefully. She watched his chest heave, up and down, as he took in air and let it out. He stirred and pulled up the cream duvet, which signaled to her that he was feeling cold. She slid out of the bed and picked up the white air-condition remote control and raised the temperature of the room. Before long, the room warmed up to a temperature that was more comfortable.

She got back into bed and her thoughts went back to about twenty-six years before when she first met Julius. They had met when Julius was serving as a youth corper, posted to Kaduna as part of the National Youth Service Corp. Julius had come to her mother's shop, which she took care of whenever her mother was not around, to buy two bars of bathing soap. As she handed him his change, she caught him staring at her with a forlorn look, like he was lost. She would later learn that his bags had been stolen from the orientation camp and the money he used was from his wallet, which sat in his black pouch along with his identity cards and other essentials.

Two weeks later, he was able to replace the lost items but still found all sorts of excuses to come to her mother's shop so they could talk. At first Zainab did not know what to make of their friendship, the only thing she knew was that she looked forward to Julius's short visits under the guise that he needed to buy a tin of powdered milk or a pack of teabags.

Whenever he came around, they would discuss his life in Lagos, his family and his future plans. This excited her and was definitely different from the things most men who came around wanted to talk about. Most of them were sons of rich merchants and ministers who took every opportunity to either brag about what their fathers were doing, or brag about what new business deal their fathers had sealed and how much money it meant they stood to inherit. What surprised her the most about the other young men that came around was the fact that they never quite spoke about themselves. She suspected it was because they had nothing to offer, so they used their only selling points: their parents' wealth.

This was one of the things that excited her about Julius. He did not have much when compared to the other men, but he had fire in his eyes, and that drive to succeed was very attractive to her. It was so attractive that when he asked her to marry him a couple of months, with nothing more than a little faded silver ring, she agreed without so much as a pause.

Her family was enraged by this development, particularly as they had pledged her hand in marriage to Ahmadu Dansaki, the state governor's son. Marriage into the Dansaki family meant that her family's fortune would be greatly enhanced because she would be marrying into wealth. What enraged her family more was the fact that he was not Muslim. Her father drummed it into her, amidst threats of disowning her, that no one in the history of their family had married an infidel, and certainly not a poor one at that.

All her siblings were also on the side of her father. It had never been done, and they would not let it happen. Her elder male siblings threatened to disfigure her and warned her that they would make her life hell on earth if she went ahead to marry Julius. It was a trying time not just for her, but for Julius as well. In fact, he began to receive death threats from other suitors, particularly Ahmadu, but she stuck with him. This was a love that was not going to fade and so, in the dead of the night of Julius's end of service parade, she escaped with him on the night bus from Kaduna to Lagos. Even though it was a risky move, she was happy she made it.

Right after they got to Lagos, they had their court marriage and started a travel agency business from their one bedroom flat and through a combination of luck and hard work, over the years they turned their business into a multi-million naira success.

As Zainab continued to reminisce, she got up from the bed, walked up to the drawer of her dressing table and pulled out a little black box from amongst the many boxes of gold, silver and diamond trinkets she had acquired over the years. She opened the box and there lay the little silver ring her husband had given to her when he proposed.

They had indeed come a long way, she thought, as she took the little box back to their bed. She looked over at Julius and saw him awake and staring at her with a sleepy smile.

"Good morning, my love. Did you sleep well?" Zainab asked.

"Yes, I did, and now I am about to have my breakfast," Julius said as he pulled her plump frame closer to himself. His left hand trailed along the path of kisses he was leaving on her neck, down her back, and his other hand made its way across her thighs, slowly brushing her centre as he ignited flames of passion within her. Even after many years and two children, he still had the power to turn her into pulp with his expert fingers and she knew how to make him go speechless with longing.

She giggled and turned around so that her face met his face. As she rubbed her nose against his, the wooden box dropped out of her hand onto the cream coloured rug. He bent over to kiss her, with the same intensity his kisses had held for her for years.

Chapter Thirty-Five

TAGGING ALONG WITH Lorraine and Ugorgi, Adaugo went along in the branch car to see a potential customer whose office was located in Ikeja. In the back seat, Lorraine was arranging her customer folders to keep all her details straight, and she looked over at Adaugo on the seat beside her. Adaugo didn't notice; she was lost in thought.

"A penny for your thoughts, young lady," Lorraine said.

"Nothing much, just thinking about this customer I have to see. I hope he opens the account. I really need to meet my target."

In reality, she was thinking of how she could combine seeing this new potential customer with seeing Julius without Lorraine noticing. She could have decided to see the new customer on a different day, but she had called Julius on the phone to inform him of her decision to go ahead with furthering her studies. Thrilled by her decision, he had asked her to come and see him that afternoon to sign some forms so that he could make a reservation for her. He sounded so enthusiastic and she could not bring herself to postpone the visit to a different day, so she agreed. She had been wondering how she was going to pull off a visit to Ikeja when she found out that Lorraine was also going to Ikeja, albeit a different area. So she decided to join Lorraine in the branch car in the guise that she was seeing a different customer who was not expecting her. Now sitting in the car, she wondered if it would not have been wiser to reschedule the visit to Julius for a different day.

"Well, if that's all you are thinking about, no problem. I don't believe you though. I have seen how the mallam who converts currencies comes to visit you every pay day. I have been monitoring you and I know you are planning something big because not long after he leaves, you go to Chuma and pay in pounds. You have been doing this for a number of months now and I have been watching you. This is a small branch so it is difficult to keep anything a secret, so spill," Lorraine urged.

Adaugo did not reply.

"What are you planning because I know we don't spend pounds in this country," Lorraine pressed with a slant of her eye brow.

Some moments of silence passed between them while Adaugo reflected on the possibility that everyone in the branch knew of her movements. She looked through the front mirror and her eyes met Ugorgi's; his were signaling that it was true.

"Oh well, since you all know something is up anyway, I guess I might as well tell you. I am planning to travel abroad. I feel really stuck in this job and I feel that this is the perfect opportunity to do it, a chance to see a different part of the world from Nigeria, develop new ideas and further my education," Adaugo confessed.

"Really? That's brilliant! Have you decided on a course of study yet?" Lorraine asked.

"Well, yes… It will be a combination of IT and Management, the best of both worlds really, considering I have an engineering background."

"I think that is impressive. I always wondered what an engineer was doing selling banking products. This job is not the best for you. I always felt you could do more, but it was not my place to say," Lorraine said.

"Life happens… and I believe that for the first time in a long time, I am finally on the right path. I wake up feeling more purposeful, you know? Like I am heading towards something finally…"

"I really admire you for taking this step. I remember when I considered going abroad. This was before I met my husband, but everyone kept telling me to get married first, have kids and then I should do it. I took their advice and shortly after, I met and got married to my husband; but sometimes I wish I hadn't because where am I now? I have three small kids and a job I absolutely hate, but I can't quit because I need the money to provide for my family. Don't get me wrong, I am thankful for my husband and kids, but sometimes I wonder how I would have turned out if I had stuck to my guns and followed my dreams." Lorraine's regret was evident in her sigh.

"But you can still pursue your dreams. The fact that you have a family shouldn't stop you," Adaugo replied.

"My dear, you are still young, you don't understand. It is going to be difficult to make any change but you have the perfect opportunity now; you have no kids, neither do you have too many responsibilities. You should do it. Who knows whether your destiny lies elsewhere? Please

183

don't be like me. I have never told my husband this because I don't want him to feel like I regret the life I have, but if I could advise myself of five years ago, I would not have gotten married. That's my cross to bear."

Adaugo thought about all Lorraine had said. Finally she replied, "Thank you for the words of encouragement. I really needed to hear that."

"Your parents must be very supportive of your dreams," Lorraine said.

"Actually, they don't have a clue about this. The only person in my family who is aware is Obioma, my sister, and she is sworn to secrecy," Adaugo laughed.

"Jesus Christ of Nazareth!!! Your parents don't know? So you are doing this alone?" Lorraine asked.

"Yes, indeed."

"That's very dangerous and courageous, but you need to tell them so they know what you are doing. What if they kick against it? You really have to tell them. It is wrong to keep it to yourself!" Lorraine said.

"I know… I plan to tell them this weekend. I wanted to make proper strides before telling them. I didn't want anyone to discourage me, like your family did to you," Adaugo said quietly.

"Now that you put it that way, I understand. Just tell them and watch how things unfold. If it is the right path for you, it will surely work out, I know it will. Let me know if you need any help with anything, okay?"

"I will, thank you." Speaking with Lorraine make Adaugo feel as though a weight had been lifted off her shoulders. She would tell her parents this weekend. It was time to rip the bandage off, once and for all.

They both settled back into silence while Ugorgi

discretely turned up the volume of the radio, now that he had heard all of their conversation. All the pieces of the puzzle and why madam was always meeting that mallam now fell into place.

I hope it goes well for madam, he thought as he took another look at Adaugo through the front mirror.

CHAPTER THIRTY-SIX

ADAUGO ARRIVED HOME on an *Okada*, a commercial motorbike, later that evening. Commercial motorbikes worked like taxis in the sense that they could be hired to travel short distances for a pre-agreed fee. A key advantage of boarding an *Okada* was that one was not encumbered by traffic jams which held other motorists. The disadvantage however, was that they were prone to accidents due to the rough manner in which operatives, desperate to drop off their existing customer to pick up a new one, rode them. No day passed by on the streets of Lagos without at least three accidents involving an *Okada*. These risks did nothing to stop people from using them as most people had few other choices. They often boarded with the hope that they would not become accident victims themselves.

Earlier that day, Adaugo had met with Mr. Omisore who had, not surprisingly, expressed happiness that she was finally "seeing the light," as he put it. He filled the forms, took copies of her passport and gave her a document which showed that he would book a flight for her when she had received her visa and decided on her actual departure date. For now, this was a step in the right

187

direction. She agreed with him and also informed him of how much she had saved. He sounded very impressed and said he wished more girls had the foresight of taking their destinies into their own hands, rather than waiting for life to happen to them. She could only silently hope that her parents would have the same outlook and excitement when she shared her news with them.

She had thanked him profusely and was excited her plans were beginning to fall into place. She had finally received and sent her transcript over to De Montfort University-Leicester about a month before and was just waiting for their decision regarding whether they would offer her an admission to study Information Systems Management.

The more she thought about the potential of experiencing a different culture and style of teaching, the more she found it hard to keep her excitement hidden. She wondered how she had managed to keep it a secret from her family these past seven months. Soon she wouldn't need to. She would call her parents and siblings, including Obioma, who would feign ignorance, and tell them of her plans. There were bound to be objections, no doubt, but she knew that the objections would have little impact in swaying her from her decision, especially with all that she had put in place. Every day she seemed to hear and see the Universe continually provide her with clues and helpful omens to help her believe beyond doubt that this was what she was to do. This was the right path.

She alighted from the commercial motorcycle, paid the cyclist 70 naira for her fare and let herself through the black gate of her house, which was now falling apart with rust, and walked through across the compound, up the stairs to the flat she shared with her family.

She pressed the doorbell and was let in by Obioma who greeted her. For a split second, Adaugo thought she saw a strange look on Obioma's face, but dismissed it as fatigue from the day. Her day had been a long one, especially as the second customer who she had gone to see had not opened the account. His reason was that the opening balance was too high. Adaugo was not too disappointed by this development. How could she be when hidden in her black faux leather handbag was a confirmation form for a free open return flight to the United Kingdom?

She made her way through the corridor and started to turn left into the room she shared with Obioma when she heard her father call out her name.

"Adaugo, *bia ebe a*, come here," her father shouted.

"*Ana m abia*, I am coming," she responded and hurried to the sitting room.

She greeted her parents and dropped her bags on the black wooden dining table which was situated behind the chair her father was sitting on, and walked towards him to face him.

"*Onwe ife mere?* Did anything happen?" Adaugo said, looking troubled.

"*Nodu ana*, sit down," Obiora replied.

She sat down and glanced at her mother, who was not betraying any emotions.

"What is this?" Obiora asked, waving a brown envelope with some white papers in it.

"I am not sure Daddy, let me see," Adaugo said as she reached across the room to her father to look at the papers.

Obiora handed over the envelope with the papers to her and waited. She opened the envelope and removed the papers. In her hands was a letter of admission from De Montfort University-Leicester. Her face brightened with joy; she was thrilled to finally receive the admission letter she had been waiting for. She must have misunderstood the email she received from the admissions team because she had expected her admission letter to come in her email. She giggled joyfully as she quickly read the contents of the letter but as she looked up, she met her father's steely gaze and eyes filled with pure fury. Her joy quickly dissipated as she heard him say, "Young lady, give me that letter and sit yourself down!"

CHAPTER THIRTY-SEVEN

"SO YOU WANT to travel outside this country, just like that? Without telling anybody *okwa ya*, is that so? You want to travel without telling anybody anything?" her father barked.

"No Daddy, I planned to get the admission first and then tell you," Adaugo replied, panicking.

Her plan to inform her family had not quite worked out the way she had planned and the fury in her father's eyes made her wonder if she had kept them out of the loop for too long.

"So you have grown so old and wise that you feel you can do anything while living under my roof because you have a job *okwa ya*, is that so? I *bu cha na, nke iji je chota* admission. You are my daughter and I would remind you that as long as you live under my roof, which I pay rent on, you will abide by my rules. You are not going anywhere!" her father continued.

Obiora started to tear the admission letter but Ngozi, who had been silent, stopped him just in time and asked to read the letter. She put on her pair of reading glasses and went through the contents of the letter.

"You will stay in this house and get married; after you

191

CHIKAMSO C. EFOBI

get married, you will move to your husband's house and bear kids, and continue your job like a woman is meant to. You have no business as a woman pursuing lofty goals and gallivanting around the world like a girl with no morals! People are supposed to see you go to work, come back on time and go into your father's house. That is how good girls should behave. A good girl should not be too ambitious or she will not find a husband! You are almost twenty-five years old. At your age, your mother already had you, Ifeoma and Obioma. We have been keeping quiet because times are a bit different with your generation. You want to finish university and start working before getting married, but this travelling to a different country and getting an advanced degree, I will not allow it! It will scare away men who want to marry you!" Obiora said.

"Daddy, why would my getting an advanced degree scare a man? Would getting a second degree suddenly turn me into a monster?" Adaugo asked.

"Stop asking me stupid questions, young lady! If you get a Master's degree and your suitors only have Bachelor's degrees, then they would feel intimidated by you because you would have more knowledge than them. The men may start to feel like they cannot control you. A man wants to be able to control his woman. That is why he is the man of the house. I have always encouraged you to pursue your dreams and speak up for yourself, but this dream is a bit too far-fetched. I don't want to end up with an unmarried spinster in my house. When you get married and have children, then you can study for your Master's anywhere in the world, with the permission of your husband," said Obiora.

"Daddy, please, don't be like this. I have done so much to make this happen. I have saved most of my salary for the past nine months in addition to some money I saved prior to this, just to make sure I am able to afford the tuition fee and I am almost there. This admission letter was the last bit I was waiting for and I planned to tell you this weekend. Please don't dash my dreams like this."

"It is like you lost your hearing. I have told you, you are going nowhere, go and find a new dream. Ngozi, give me that letter!" Obiora shouted.

"*Biko*, please don't tear it," Ngozi said as he handed over the letter to her husband.

"Please reconsider," Adaugo urged. "I don't plan to be a wayward woman. I just want to be happy and this job is not making me happy. Prior to catching this dream, I had been drowning myself in food. Food was the only thing that gave me joy, but since I have been putting things in place, I have been so energetic and joyful that somehow my life is not over in this dead end job. Please reconsider! I have already done so much work. I also got a free flight ticket from one of my customers and all that is left is to accept the admission, raise the rest of the money, and I can go. I am sorry I did not tell you earlier. I am really sorry." Adaugo was in tears but her father appeared to be unaffected by them.

As her husband stormed out of the room, Ngozi looked at Adaugo who was now crying uncontrollably and said quietly, "I *ma na I kari gwa m*, you should have told me of your plans."

"I wanted to, I really planned to this weekend," she replied, sobbing.

"You should have at least told me when you started

making the plans, so at least I would know beforehand. Now your father is so angry and I don't know if he can ever change his mind. He doesn't get angry often, but you could see how he was fuming."

"Please, can you talk to him for me? Please, *Nne biko*, mother, please talk to him. I really want to go," Adaugo replied.

"I will try; I seriously doubt it will work. Don't worry, if this is the right path for you, things will work out; that is my belief. *Ngwa* clean your eyes, look at your white camisole, you have ruined it with mascara and make up. Clean your eyes; God is in control," her mother said, going over to Adaugo to comfort her. But even as she held her daughter she thought about the fact that she had had exactly the same experience over thirty years ago.

She remembered the feeling she experienced when she brought her O Level results home with her and announced to her parents that she wanted to study law. She was immediately discouraged and told that an unmarried woman had no place being a lawyer because it would scare suitors away. Her father quickly recommended a more feminine career – teaching food and nutrition to secondary school students – which she eventually took because she wanted to be a good daughter. She knew all too well of that sinking feeling, that feeling of confusion and hopelessness; she knew exactly how her daughter was feeling right now because even though she had finally studied law after having five kids and eventually became a lawyer, it took so much from her to balance losing a child, running a home and going to work that sometimes she wondered if she may have been better off if she had pursued the career she actually wanted many years ago.

CHAPTER THIRTY-EIGHT

WAS ALL THIS work for nothing? These were Adaugo's thoughts as she reported for work the next morning, feeling very little like her usual self. The conversation with her father from the night before lingered at the edges of her mind, and when she thought on it for too long a feeling of hopelessness crept in and threatened to drown her.

All of the nice outfits she had denied herself, all of the things her friends had been enjoying which she had skipped out on in order to save, like new blackberry phones, trips to the beach, dinners out, all of these things had been at the expense of saving for her future. *And now, where has it gotten me? To a dead end? What was it all for?*

Hot tears filled her eyes and panic set in. She let the tears run freely and didn't try to stop them. The more she thought about it, all of it, the sacrifices and the words with her father, the more heavily the tears seemed to flow. All the pent up frustration of keeping her plans to herself, all in a bid to make it work, was beginning to show itself in a flood of grief down her cheeks.

A thought came to her about her makeup and the fact

that her colleagues would soon arrive, but at that point, she did not care. They would come in and see her tear-streaked face; they would know she had failed and that she was hopeless, and she didn't care. Mostly, she just felt tired.

If she was at home, she would have slept after such a good cry, but she couldn't. She walked to the staff toilet instead and tore some tissue off the white roll and wiped her tears. As she wiped the tears, even more tears began to surge from her eyes. So she took out the entire roll and walked slowly to back to her seat. As she sat down, she heard Herself ask, "Why are you crying, young woman? Why all these tears?"

"Because it is all hopeless," she replied, blubbering into the tissue.

"Why do you think it is hopeless? It is just a little bump in the road," Herself replied.

"A little bump? A little bump? Did you not hear what my father said? I am not going anywhere. I should find a new dream," she replied with a sigh.

"I heard, I was there, but instead of hearing the no, I understood that he is worried. Your father is just worried. His concerns were valid. First of all, you didn't tell him about your plans. Think about it this way. Imagine if you had a daughter living under the same roof with you and the only way you find out she is planning to leave the country is by opening a letter. How would you feel?" Herself asked.

"But I planned to tell him tomorrow. He would not have found out if he did not open my letter," Adaugo protested.

"Yes, that is true. We both know that is true, but he is

not in your heart. So he is not working with the same information that both of us are working with, and that's the difference. Look at it this way, his idea of happiness is seeing you married. He has no other picture of happiness for you and this is not his fault. It is not your fault that you want more. He is just worried about the safety of his beloved daughter and all these thoughts are now manifesting as anger. Every regular human being just wants to be understood and once you can understand the underlying reason behind people's reactions, then you are able to empathise with them and even reason with them," Herself said.

Adaugo had stopped crying as she listened.

"Don't worry about this. It will all work out. Remember, when you want something, all of the universe conspires in helping you to achieve it," Herself said.

"The universe better work quickly because according to what I read yesterday from the admission letter, I have just one month to accept the admission," she said.

"Replace fear with curiosity, replace anxiety with love," came the reply from Herself.

"What does that mean?" Adaugo asked, but Herself kept quiet.

"Replace fear with curiosity, replace anxiety with love," she repeated. As she pondered over these words, she heard her mobile phone buzz. She picked it up and looked at the screen, it was Wale.

"Hey you… How are you doing," Adaugo said, trying to sound cheerful.

"I am okay," Wale said from the other end of the line. "You don't sound okay. Are you alright?"

"I am not alright, but don't worry about it," she

replied.

"Of course I would be worried. Tell me, what is it?" Wale continued to ask, concerned.

She told him then what had transpired the evening before. When she was done speaking, he asked what universities she had applied to and what courses. She told him. Before ending the call, Wale invited her to the wedding of two of his office colleagues, Chidi and Adunni, both of whom had met at work and were getting married after dating secretly for about a year. Wale went on to explain that even though the couple thought their relationship was a secret, everyone knew. Their discrete touches when they thought no one was looking had not gone unnoticed. Their church wedding was taking place the following weekend.

"How come you are not going with Kemi, your girlfriend?" Adaugo inquired.

"She has an audition so she cannot make it and it sounds like you could do with a pick me up. You sound husky, like a man," Wale teased.

"You are not serious. Okay, I will make it. What time should I be ready to go?" she asked.

"Be ready at 10am, I will pick you up by then. The wedding starts at 11am," he replied.

"Alright then, see you next Saturday," she said.

"See you then, and cheer up, okay?" Wale said.

"I will," Adaugo replied and put down the phone.

Wale put down the phone, opened his laptop and typed the words, De Montfort University-Leicester into the Google search bar. Within some seconds, the results came up and he picked up his warm mug of Nescafe and began to read through the contents of his laptop screen.

Chapter Thirty-Nine

TEN MINUTES EARLY, Wale pulled up in front of Adaugo's house and took out his keys from the ignition of his black Toyota Camry saloon car. He was immaculately dressed in a white Babariga outfit, a brown, embroidered traditional cap with white patterns and a pair of brown leather shoes. Even the coolness of the air conditioner could not stop him from feeling the effects of the hot Nigerian sun. He wiped his face with his white handkerchief, stepped out of the car and examined his outfit in the driver's window of his car. When he was convinced he looked like he meant to, he took out his mobile phone from his pocket and called Adaugo. The phone rang a number of times before she picked up.

"Hello, Wale you are here, already?" she sounded breathless and he could picture her scampering around and rushing to finish getting ready.

"Yes I am, why are you sounding rushed? Don't tell me you are not ready. We had an agreement," Wale said, sounding annoyed.

"I am sorry, I'm running a bit late. But it won't take me long to be ready. I just got out of the shower but you can come in, Obioma will get you something to drink so you can cool down a bit. It is very hot outside," Adaugo replied.

"Don't bribe me with a drink. Hurry up!" Wale said and ended the call.

When he got to their front door, Obioma opened the door and let him in and offered him a drink. She sat with him and made small talk while Adaugo finished dressing. When she finally did emerge from her bedroom, she looked beautiful in a brown and white lace, traditional long skirt which hugged her figure perfectly, coupled with a long sleeved blouse with a v-neckline. She had let her braids down and paired the outfit with a silver shoe and bag set. Wale looked at her and gulped; he had never seen her look this beautiful or dressed so well for any occasion. He had only ever seen her dressed casually, or for work.

"You look great Adaugo; really, really nice," Wale managed to say when he regained his composure.

"Thank you. You look really good too. It looks like we have coordinated colours," she said, smiling. She stood there admiring him and looking at both the similar colours in the outfits they had chosen.

"I aim to please, imagine the coincidence! Perhaps you snuck into my house last night to check what outfit I was wearing so you could coordinate with me," Wale joked.

"Yeah, right... Let's go, we are running late, aren't we?" Adaugo laughed.

Obioma saw them off to the gate and they got into Wale's hot car. Adaugo immediately began complaining about needing to let some hot air out and Wale did not argue. He quickly started the ignition and rolled down the windows.

As they made their way through the streets of Mushin and onto Isolo road, she tried hard to mask the attraction she felt for Wale. Over the years she had learned to suppress it, but today she was not sure why all these emotions and such a strong attraction were coming to the forefront. Perhaps it was the fact that he was so immaculately dressed in his traditional outfit. Or was it the way his fingers inadvertently brushed her thighs as he shifted gears? She needed to distract herself.

"How is Kemi?" Adaugo asked, breaking the silence.

"She is doing great. I suspect that she may be at the venue of her audition now. I haven't spoken to her today," Wale replied.

There was another uncomfortable silence and Wale took the opportunity to find out whether Adaugo's dad had changed his mind and acquiesced for her to travel.

"No, he hasn't. He is quite adamant that he does not want to speak about it. It is all beginning to look hopeless, Wale," she sighed.

"How long do you have to accept the offer?" he asked.

"Just two weeks. I hope something changes soon."

"Perhaps your mum could speak to him," Wale suggested.

"Yes, she has tried, but she said he was not budging," Adaugo replied, unable to hide the sadness and frustration in her voice.

"After accepting the offer, what next?" Wale asked.

"I would have to send my school fees over to the university through a telegraphic transfer, the university would confirm receipts of the funds, and I would then leave my maintenance funds in my account for 3 months. During that time I should receive a certificate of sponsorship from the university. It is this certificate of sponsorship, along with my bank statements, offer letter and completed application form I would submit to the embassy to get a visa," she explained.

"It sounds like we still have a long way to go. We just have to be hopeful. That's all we can do. I strongly believe that you didn't do all this work for nothing. Something will change soon and if not, you may have to make the decision to go ahead without your father's permission. After all, you are a grown woman," Wale said.

"I have thought about doing that but I don't want to do it yet, because it may be disrespectful to my father. I see where he is coming from though. He doesn't want me to wake up in ten to fifteen years' time, an educated and unmarried woman with no children, when my mates will be thinking of what universities to enroll *their* children to. He doesn't want me to lose out on life. I nurse those fears too from time to time; but the thing is, if I don't pursue my heart's desire, I may have already lost out on life because I won't be living as my authentic self. I would be living someone else's life plan....You know what, let's talk about something else. This topic is getting a bit depressing. How is work going?"

"Work is great. We just secured a huge deal to supply petroleum products to a huge telecoms firm. Let's just say my manager is very pleased with me right now."

They continued conversing and getting caught up as Wale navigated the road through Ojuelegba, on to Surulere, where the wedding reception was taking place. The traffic was moving at a steady pace as they got on to Bode Thomas road. All of a sudden a light blue, RAV 4 jeep honked noisily behind them and sped past them, cutting through oncoming traffic. Wale had to quickly swerve to left to avoid a collision with the errant vehicle.

"What was that?" Adaugo screamed, disturbed by the near collision.

"I really wonder where he or she was rushing to! We almost got hit!" Wale said, trying to gain his composure.

They got to their destination and while Wale was looking for a good parking spot to park the car, Adaugo spotted the same jeep which had sped past them some minutes ago. The driver was also parking, right across from them.

"What do you know? Look at that silly guy that sped past us like a mad man! He is also just parking! So after all his flying, he still got here the same time as us," Adaugo exclaimed.

"Just imagine that! He would have hit us in his haste. What a mental case!" Wale responded, still obviously upset by the incident.

"Pay him no mind. Let's go in," Adaugo said in a soothing voice as they got out of the car.

As they walked into the reception hall, Adaugo heard Herself say, "You know girl, this incident with the speeding jeep says so much about life. Sometimes people seem to be doing better than you. They may seem to be way ahead of you in hitting some goals that you may not be close to achieving, but never be bothered by it. Just keep on working hard and carrying on with the steady pace that works best for you. Never be jealous nor be concerned about their apparent speedier progress and before long, like the case of the speeding jeep, you will find yourself at the same level of achievement. The difference is that you will have hit your goals in a way that best suits you and promotes your peace of mind. Everyone has a race to run, but not everyone races at the same speed. The important thing is to keep putting one foot before the other, and keep working hard to get to the finish line."

"Fascinating!" Adaugo exclaimed.

"Did you say something?" Wale asked.

"No nothing… I was just thinking out loud," Adaugo replied, smiling to herself.

Chapter Forty

T IMOTHY ADEBAYO SAT in the seat of his well-decorated office. He had just received a call from the regional manager who wanted to follow up about his execution of one of the outcomes of a recent meeting. The meeting had started off as usual with the meeting secretary going through the actions from the last meeting, after which they went through the usual agenda items, how the different branch balance sheets were faring in comparison with their targets.

When they were done reporting results and plans for the next month, the regional manager, Mr. Ibe, brought up a different item which was not included in the agenda. The retail segment of their owning group had taken a hit due to some poor investment decisions taken by management and as a result, they needed to look for ways to start cutting costs. Some options such as changing suppliers to more affordable ones and reinforcing smart printing had been discussed at the group level, but by the end of the meeting they had all come to the same bitter conclusion: if they wanted to hit their cost savings targets, they would need to reduce their workforce by 10%, starting with the newest of staff.

Their reasoning was that new staff were most likely young people with fewer responsibilities and most of their lives ahead of them. They would very easily get new jobs elsewhere, as opposed to those who had been with the bank for decades. As expected, this news was greeted with mass hysteria across the room. Mr. Ibe asked his managers to quickly identify their new staff who fit the criteria and have meetings with them as soon as possible, within the following week. Now he was checking with Timothy to see how things were going with accomplishing this new, important task.

"I will get right on it, sir," Timothy Adebayo replied and ended the call.

He heaved a sigh, and picked up the office internal phone. He did not like what he was about to do.

"Adaugo, can you come into my office briefly?" Mr. Adebayo asked.

"Certainly, boss. I will be with you right away." She replied.

Timothy replaced the phone in the receiver and rubbed his hand across his face and over his bald head. In all his fifteen years of working, he had only needed to fire someone once and that was one of his former drivers for gross misconduct. The driver had no scruples using the official car to visit his numerous girlfriends, so firing the driver had been a relatively easy and utterly satisfying thing to do.

This was different. This was a hardworking young woman who was trying to make a life for herself. Even though he had been mean to her in the past, he never meant any word he had said to her during the team meetings. It was all part of the job – it was expected of him to be tough and ruthless so as to reduce the possibility of slackness amongst his staff, and it had worked. She had been meeting her monthly targets and she even seemed happier, as if the many lectures he'd given her had filled her with more energy to do her work.

Now he was about to give her the unpleasant news that she was going to lose her job. He wished there was something he could do to spare her from this predicament, but his hands were tied. He needed to do this or his job would be on the line. Oh, how he hated this!

"Mr. Adebayo, you asked for me?" Adaugo said peering into the office from the doorway.

"Yes, Adaugo. Come in, please take a seat," Timothy Adebayo said, faking a smile.

"Wait… Run this past me again. You are losing your job? How is this possible?" Ngozi asked her daughter, surprised by the news her daughter had just given her.

"Apparently the bank is going through financial difficulty and they have decided that in order to cut costs, they need to let some staff go, starting with the newest of staff. I have been given one month's notice so I get my salary for this month and next month, and I get paid for all the holidays I have not taken this year, which equates to about three months of pay," Adaugo replied, taking off her shoes and unbuttoning her suit jacket.

"Were you the only one affected in your branch?" her mother asked.

"Yes, I am the newest staff and I fit the criteria perfectly. Mr. Adebayo sounded very pained and he offered to give me a glowing reference if I ever needed it. He kept reassuring me that it had nothing to do with my performance," she replied.

"*Nawo o,*... And you said you would get the equivalent of three months of pay?" her mother asked.

"Yes, three months. This month I will get my regular pay and at the end of next month, I will get paid for two months," Adaugo explained again.

"When do you have to start your Master's programme?" Ngozi asked.

"Roughly three months' time."

Ngozi got up and paced around the house. She usually did this when she was in deep thought. Adaugo stared at her in silence as she did this. She knew better than to interrupt her mother whenever she was thinking deeply. Finally some minutes of complete silence, Ngozi said, "*Nne*... What I know is that all things work together for good for those that love God. If I was unsure about this your studying abroad project in the past, now I am 100% convinced. How else we explain to ourselves how you just lost this job at a time which perfectly aligns with when you are supposed to accept your admission? This is the Creator taking away any back up plan you had and actively pushing you along the path you are meant to be on."

Adaugo considered this for a while and the more she considered it, the more it all made perfect sense to her. More than that, she heard Herself in that moment, saying, "Trust that everything happens for a reason, even though we are not always wise enough to see it."

Chapter Forty-One

O N THE AFTERNOON of her leaving party, Adaugo sat on the bed she shared with her sister Obioma and tried to organise her outfits, which were currently in a heap on her bed, into her two suitcases. The past three months had passed more quickly than she expected and had been filled with many last minute activities, such as having to make many trips to the market to buy outfits, underwear and other items, like as a winter jacket, at the insistence of her mother. She had tried so many times without success to convince her mother that she didn't need a winter jacket just yet, particularly as she was going to be arriving in the United Kingdom in the month of September, but Ngozi was having none of that. Her mother had heard tales of how cold it was abroad and had decided that there was no way her daughter was going to freeze in a foreign country. So, they combed the streets of Tejuosho market in search of a jacket that suited Ngozi's taste and when they finally did, Adaugo was beyond relieved.

The monstrosity was a brown leather coat with faux wool around the collar and Adaugo had no doubt that it would be more suitable for someone heading to the Arctic

Circle for the winter. She knew already that there was no chance in hell she was ever going to be caught dead wearing that, but to please her mother she smiled and pretended that it was the best gift ever.

Now she picked up the jacket and stuffed it into her hand luggage, which was now almost completely filled up with just the one item.

As she continued packing her outfits, she cast her mind back to the series of events and all of the coincidences which had led to this very moment.

After she informed her mother about the loss of her job, she started to really wrestle with the possibility that she would go ahead to accept the admission without her father's consent. At the time she saw this as the only way, especially as she was sure beyond any inkling of a doubt that this was the right path for her. If not, why else had she lost the one thing - her job -- which served as her only insurance, her fail safe option if the plans to travel fell through? Her father had actually told her to focus on the job. Now it was no more. She never was one to believe in coincidences. Everything happens for a reason and this was not going to be an exception.

Then, as she laid in bed that night, she decided that if by Monday, three days later, she had not heard anything positive from her father about changing his mind on his stance, she would send an email to the admissions officer accepting the admission. Let all hell break loose, she thought. She would never forget how she felt on the Sunday, the day before she was to accept the admission, when her dad came into her room. She had been listening to some music on her worn out mobile phone, which she did not want to replace because she had been saving to study abroad. Hearing a knock on the door, she turned off the music in time to hear her father's voice requesting to be let in. She immediately went to the door and unlocked it, muttered greetings, let him in, and went back to lie down in bed. Since she informed her mum about the news of her losing her job, her father had not said anything so she assumed he was there to extract more details from her about the job loss.

Her father wasted no time in telling her his purpose for coming to see her. "Here, this is for you," he had said, handing a paper to her which she recognised immediately.

"I have decided that you should go ahead and accept the admission. You have done a lot of work on this already, especially with your denying yourself all these many months of things your mates have been enjoying because you want to pursue this dream of yours. I thought about it and I came to the conclusion that I would be a bad father if I denied you this opportunity. After all, I have strived with your mother to raise all of you as independent thinkers," her father said.

Adaugo could not believe what she was hearing. "Daddy, do you mean I can go?" she said with tears streaming down her face.

"Yes, you can, on one condition," Obiora replied with a straight face.

"Anything Daddy, anything just tell me what it is," Adaugo replied excitedly.

"You must make contact with us, particularly your mother, each day. I do not want her to ever worry about your well-being. We have no relatives and no friends in this country you are going to, but we trust that God will keep you safe, especially as He has revealed to us through recent happenings that this is the right thing for you to do," her father instructed.

"No problem, Dad, I will make contact with you and Mum every single day. Thank you for changing your mind. You don't know how much this means to me," Adaugo replied, her face filled with tears of joy.

"*Ngwa*, now clean your face. Stop crying and come out of this room. Let us watch the news together," her father replied.

She could feel the tears forming in her eyes as she cast her mind back to that day. It was now almost all a distant history. By this time tomorrow, she would be en route to the airport about to get on a flight which would lead her to a new life as a student in a country which only seemed like a distant dream a year ago.

At 2:00pm she had packed her two suitcases, and then had to repack one of them in order to make space for another of the yellow wrappers her mother had brought into the room.

"It is for the cold, my daughter. You never know, you may need it," her mother had said.

Adaugo was very sure she would not need both wrappers, so she packed one and kept the spare one in the wardrobe, along with some of her old outfits her mum had brought just in case.

At this rate, I will need four suitcases if I keep packing all these items, she thought as she hid the yellow wrapper at the bottom of a "Ghana must go" woven bag in her wardrobe.

There was a quick knock on the door and Obioma walked in. "Uncle Nkem just gave Daddy a call saying that he was on his way with Aunty and the kids. Have you taken your bath? I don't think they would appreciate seeing their star girl still in pajamas at 2 o' clock in the afternoon!"

"I will soon be done. Come and assist me in lifting these suitcases from the bed," Adaugo beckoned.

As they both struggled to lift the suitcases off the bed, Obioma said, "You know I am very proud of you."

"Why do you say so?" Adaugo answered with surprise.

"You had a dream and you worked silently till you achieved it. Remember that day Anozie called me to persuade you to drop the idea? I was very skeptical and I didn't think you could actually pull it off, but you did."

"It is not that big a deal. Anyone can decide to travel abroad. You just need to identify a course of study, pay for it, apply for a visa and you are off!" she replied.

"But most of the people you refer to have had these things paid for by their parents or wealthy relatives. You actually saved most of your salary, had the courage to end a relationship with a partner who was not supportive of your dream, and even almost defied your father. It takes a lot of guts. Many people have quit in the face of much less. You will be the first person in our entire family, extended family included, to have achieved this and I think you should be proud of yourself," Obioma argued.

"Well… but I didn't do it all by myself…." Adaugo started to say.

"Stop arguing and accept it. I am proud of you," Obioma said, hugging her only sister.

"Thank you, hearing that means a lot to me," Adaugo replied.

"Okay… enough with the mushiness, go and take

your bath. Uncle Nkem will be here shortly," Obioma said with a straight face.

Two hours later, the sitting room of their flat had been filled with visitors including extended family members who were within Lagos, her colleagues from the bank, friends from university and her parents' friends. Soft drinks and alcohol were served freely by her brother Ugonna and Obiageri, their house help, while Obioma, Adaugo, Ivie and Tola made sure that the guests had enough to eat. There was *jollof* rice, fried rice, pounded yam, *eba*, *egusi* soup and *ofe onugbu*. Only one person was missing – Wale.

Adaugo was getting impatient. She assumed he was running late at first, but after two hours of repeatedly stretching her neck to see if his car was pulling up in front of the gate of her house, she decided to give him a call. The phone rang for a while and just when she was about to end the call, he picked up.

"Where are you? Everyone is here. Ivie and Tola have been asking after you," Adaugo said, trying to control the anger which was now almost reaching boiling point.

"I am sorry Ada, but I don't think I can make it. I am stuck at home babysitting my nephews. My sister just dumped them at my place at the last minute," Wale replied.

"Bring them with you. Put them in the car and bring them with you. Don't do this to me. I don't want to leave tomorrow without at least seeing you," Adaugo said with panic rising in her voice.

"Ada, I really cannot make it. Shade will expect to pick up her kids at my house and I don't want her to start driving through the traffic on the way to your house to pick them up," Wale replied.

"You have got to be kidding me, Wale. So this is how you want me to leave, without seeing you?" she replied.

"Don't make it sound like that, it is not like you are dying. I will call you later in the day to find out how the party went and will call you tomorrow before you fly. We will still keep in touch when you arrive, so all is well," Wale replied.

Adaugo ended the call feeling angry. *How could Wale not make it? After all these years of being so close?*

She tried to understand and empathise with him but try as she may, she could not stop thinking that with a little more effort on his part, Wale could have made it to the party. Her thoughts were interrupted by the sound of the clinking of a spoon against a glass.

"It is time for the toast," her father called out, and all the guests began to gather around him.

Her anger with Wale would have to wait, for now. She made her way to her father's side.

CHAPTER FORTY-TWO

T HE FOLLOWING EVENING, the group set off for the airport in two cars. The first car was driven by Obiora, with Ngozi at the front and Adaugo, Obioma and her other two siblings at the back, while Uncle Nkem, his wife, Ivie, Tola and the couple's two kids sat in the other car and followed them closely. Ivie and Tola had slept over the night before. The three girls spent the night on the brown rug in the sitting room and stayed up that night until the early hours of the following day trading stories, reminiscing and giggling over the mischievous things they had done over the years. It was not until 1:00am that Ngozi came out of the room and beckoned them to go to bed, and reminded them they had a long day ahead.

They finally did go to bed, but not before they traded a few more funny stories, laughing quietly so as not to wake Adaugo's mother.

Adaugo's phone beeped. It was a text message from Wale.

"Are you guys on your way?"

Adaugo replied, "What do you care? *Please*, leave me alone!"

A reply text came in some seconds later, "But I have apologised. At least pick up the phone so I can speak to you."

"What do you want to say again? Will you suddenly undo the fact that you didn't show up yesterday even though you had promised to come?"

"I am sorry," Wale replied.

"Okay," Adaugo replied.

Her phone rang again, it was Wale calling. She ignored the call until the phone stopped ringing.

"But you are still not picking up. Would you really leave without talking to me?" Wale texted.

"Maybe…"

They arrived at the drop-off point of Murtala Muhammed Airport and Obioma, Ivie and Tola helped Adaugo pull out her suitcases from the booth of her father's car, after which her father and Uncle Nkem drove away to the parking area to look for parking spaces.

They had arrived four hours ahead of her flight, which was at 7:00pm, because Ngozi kept insisting they must leave the house early in case they encountered any traffic on the way. She also reasoned that even if they did not encounter any traffic on the way, there might be a long queue of intending students at the airport. "It is always better to arrive too early than too late…" she reasoned.

As they passed the men dressed in military outfits at the entrance of the airport, Adaugo's mobile phone started to ring again. It was Wale.

"Are you going to get that?" Ivie asked with an inquisitive look on her face.

"Hold this for me…" Adaugo said to Ivie, handing her hand luggage over to her.

"What can I do for you?" Adaugo said in an angry tone.

"You are still angry? I have said I am sorry. My hands were tied," Wale pleaded.

"You don't get it do you? In about three hours or so I will be heading off and I won't even get the chance to say goodbye to you face-to-face. It is very painful to me," she said.

"I understand and I will make it up to you," Wale said reassuringly.

"How exactly do you plan to?" Adaugo asked.

"I will think of something. Maybe I will pay you a visit when you are settled. Perhaps during the summer holidays. Trust me, we will work something out. Have you checked in now?" Wale said.

"No I haven't. We just arrived and I have a feeling we have arrived too early, thanks to my mum and her pushy ways. I guess we will wait around a bit, get some snacks to eat and then start to check-in in about an hour," Adaugo said.

"I will miss you when you go. There will be no one to call in the middle of the night or whenever, just to talk about anything and everything," Wale sighed.

"You know I will be one call away, we can still talk whenever you want," Adaugo tried to comfort him.

"No worries… I will call you in about two hours, by then you should have checked in," Wale said.

"Okay, that's fine. Let me run along now," Adaugo replied.

She ended the call and went back to join her party, her father and Uncle Nkem were now with the group.

"Are you okay?" her father asked sensing something

wrong in her mood.

"I am okay…just withdrawal symptoms," she lied.

"Alright, let us go to one of the shops and get some nibbles to eat. It looks like we have arrived too early," Obiora said and led the group to a shop where they bought plastic bottles of soft drinks and packs of fruit cake. They found an empty set of plastic seats where they sat down to eat their snacks.

"Remember your promise to your father and me. You will make contact with us every day so we know you are okay. You don't want me to worry about your well-being," Ngozi said.

"Yes Mum, I will reach out every day so you know I am alive," Adaugo replied.

Her response caused the others to let out a suppressed giggle and Adaugo turned over to her friends and they continued to discuss. After about an hour, they heard the announcement that check in had begun for her flight, so they all stood and walked towards the right gate to join a queue of prospective students which had already formed a line.

She got to the customs officers who were searching people's bags and lifted both her suitcases to be searched. When the officers were satisfied that she carried no contrabands, they asked for tips for their service.

"*I no get madam*, I don't have. Maybe next time," she said with an innocent smile.

"*Na so una dey* talk, that is what you all say. Carry on. Have a safe trip," the customs officer said, feigning anger.

"Thank you, madam," Adaugo said as she locked up her suitcases and pulled them down from the table, making way for the next passenger to be searched.

She then located the right check-in desk and proceeded to the one marked "BA Desk 21".

"Good evening madam, can I have your ticket?" The pretty lady asked.

"Yes sure…" Adaugo replied, handing over her passport and flight ticket. The lady looked at it and asked, "Will this be your first time?"

"Yes indeed…my first time," Adaugo replied excitedly.

The woman checked the weight of her suitcases and when she was done, Adaugo went back to her party.

Two hours later, Wale called and they said their good byes. "Please call me once you land, okay?" Wale said.

"Yes, sure I will. How come your environment sounds noisy?" Adaugo asked.

"I am at the petrol filling station. Text me when you get on the plane," Wale said.

"No worries…will do. Extend my greetings to Kemi," she said.

Wale hesitated before responding, "I will let her know."

Adaugo felt a knot in her heart at the end of the call. She was really going to miss her closest friend. Over the years they had formed a very close bond and she was comfortable telling him anything. He also was comfortable sharing his secrets with her. She cast her mind back to the first time they met and laughed at the memory. She had been too scared to take their relationship any further because she knew that if they messed that up, she would have no one. She remembered the look on his face when she said no to his request for them to start a relationship. He was filled with pure hurt

223

and she wished she could hug him and tell him how she really felt about him, but she was scared. Now she felt she had lost the chance. Had she done the right thing? Perhaps she should have taken the chance when she had it. Over the years they had both been with different people, but somehow she kept comparing them to him. Even when she was with Anozie, there were some days she wished he would laugh at her jokes the way Wale did or say something silly the way Wale would, instead of being so serious. Now it was too late. Perhaps they would have actually messed things up. It was best this way, she convinced herself.

Finally it was time to go through security and she said her good byes to her family and her two friends and promised to keep in touch. As she walked towards the security gates, she felt a few tears form in her eyes, but she was going to be strong she had decided and so she brushed them quickly away. This was what she wanted, she was going to pursue her dreams. Who knew where the road of life would take her?

After she went through security, she sat on the one of the seats, pulled out her phone and plugged in her headphones and selected "Only time" by Enya.

She settled into the seat and listened to the lyrics of the song:

"Who can say where the road goes?
Where the day flows?
Only time

And who can say if your love grows
As your heart chose?
Only time"

It suddenly hit her as to how perfect this song was to her present situation. Only time would tell what would happen.

> *"Who can say why your heart sighs*
> *As your love flies?*
> *Only time*
> *And who can say why your heart cries*
> *When your love lies?*
> *Only time*
> *Who can say when the roads meet*
> *That love might be in your heart?*
> *And who can say when the day sleeps*
> *If the night keeps all your heart,*
> *Night keeps all your heart?"*

As she listened, she felt a light tap on her shoulder and ignored it at first, concluding that it must have been a mistake from one of the other passengers sitting around her. She was not sure if it was her mind playing tricks on her, but she thought she had heard a man's voice calling her name.

She quickly pulled out her headphones from her ears and sat up and her eyes met Wale's smiling eyes.

"What the hell are you doing here?" she asked, blinking to make sure her eyes were not deceiving her.

He just carried on smiling like she had said nothing. She quickly reached out to touch his arm. Yes he was real, she was not dreaming it.

He laughed at her confusion and finally said, "I am also travelling to the United Kingdom, with you actually."

"How is that possible? Wale, what do you mean?" Adaugo replied, her voice slightly raised now due to her confusion.

"Shhhh, lower your voice, people are beginning to look," Wale said as he sat down beside her.

"What do you mean lower your voice? I need answers!" Adaugo replied.

"I am also going to the United Kingdom with you. I figured I had lost you in the past and now that you are actually leaving the country, I could not bear to lose you again so I told my Manager I wanted to resign so I could go and do my MBA in the UK, but he wouldn't have it. We eventually agreed that I would go on a one year study leave, after which I would return to my old company and depending on how well I did, I may be promoted. I guess it was the new deal I won for them that made them not want to let me go. So here I am," Wale explained.

"I still cannot believe this, you are also travelling to study because of me?" Adaugo asked.

"Well…technically yes, you inspired me, but I figured there was no better time than now to obtain further education and perhaps gain some inspiration and business ideas from a different part of the world," Wale responded.

"Which university are you going to?" she asked.

"De Montfort University-Leicester," Wale replied with a wink.

Finally it began to make sense why he kept asking questions wanting to know what universities she was applying to and what her plans were. Back then she thought he was just being caring and she had no way of knowing he was hatching a parallel and cunning plan to apply and travel with her.

"What about Kemi? How does she feel about this? Surely she will not be impressed that you are jetting out of the country with another woman," Adaugo said.

"We broke up about three months ago when she pieced together that I was planning to travel because of you. She said she could not compete with that. I kept it from you because I did not feel I needed to tell you back then," Wale said.

"I don't know how I feel about this Wale, honestly," Adaugo responded.

"At a point I thought it was a crazy idea, but a part of me asked what I had to lose. I searched myself and I found out that I had nothing to lose. You are the one I want to be with. I have fought these feelings for years, tried to convince myself that I would forget about these feelings, but I was just kidding myself. I have compared you to everyone I have been with and after a while I had to stop kidding myself and make the bold move again. I know you love me, I see the way you look at me. Why don't you just get rid of this fear that is holding you back? You know we would make a good team. We don't have to start anything right away, we can start slow till you are comfortable enough to trust that we would not break. All I know is that I want to be with you with every muscle and atom in my body, and I will do my best to make you happy. I have had eight years of training in the art," Wale finally finished.

There was an announcement for passengers waiting for their flight to make their way to proceed to the boarding gate. As they got up, Adaugo put her hands into Wale's and marveled at how they fit perfectly together.

"I accept, Wale…" she said.

227

Wale bent down and kissed her forehead, and said, "You will not regret this. We will be very happy together."

Adaugo had no doubt about this. She felt a huge sense of peace fill her as they handed over their boarding passes to the lady and boarded the plane. In that moment she knew that anyone could have anything they have ever wanted. All they have to do is dare to dream.

THE END

EPILOGUE

A WARRIOR OF the light always does something out of the ordinary. He may dance in the street as he walks to work. Or look into the eyes of a stranger and speak of love at first sight. From time to time, a warrior puts forward an idea which may sound ridiculous, but which he believes in.

The warriors of the light allow themselves such days.

He is not afraid to weep over old grievances, or to marvel at new discoveries. When he feels the time is right, he leaves everything behind and goes after the dream he has longed for. When he understands that he is at the limits of his resistance, he withdraws from the combat, without blaming himself for having committed one or two unexpected reckless acts.

A warrior does not spend his days trying to act out the part that others have chosen for him.

Taken from "Warrior of the Light: A Manual" by Paulo Coelho

OTHER TITLES MENTIONED IN THIS BOOK

COELHO, P. (1998). *The alchemist*. [San Francisco],
HarperSanFrancisco.

CLASON, G. (2002). *The richest man in babylon – The
success secrets of the ancients*. [New York], Penguin
Putnam Inc/ First published in 1926